BRATVA'S STOLEN BRIDE

EVIE ROSE

Copyright © 2025 by Evie Rose

All rights reserved.

No part of this book may be reproduced in any form or by any electronic or mechanical means, including information storage and retrieval systems, without written permission from the author, except for the use of brief quotations in a book review.

This story is a work of fiction. Names, characters, places, and incidents are the product of the author's imagination or are used fictitiously. Any resemblance to actual events, locales, or persons, living or dead, is coincidental.

Cover: © 2024 by Artscandare.

1

PAYTON

A hand clamps over my mouth, and a voice says, "Easy, printsessa!"

I scream, but it's already muffled completely.

My brain stutters. Another hand grabs me. I throw myself away from the man, but I'm surprised and overpowered. My eyes are wide, desperately searching for someone and there's no one to see—I'm on my way to university early, and this residential street is quiet—apart from a nondescript white van.

Struggling, kicking, I'm dragged back and a door slams shut as fabric is shoved over my head. An engine roars and the vehicle accelerates, putting me off balance, but I'm held tight as terror explodes in me.

I fight. I'm a hissing, scratching wildcat, intent on escape, even against all the odds.

This can't be happening.

But they have all the advantages. Fingers bite into my wrists and ankles, and I can't see. My bag is yanked from my shoulder and my keys and phone from the pockets of my shorts.

I'm pushed into a seat, and my wrists are tied.

In the dark, I'm totally disoriented. Fear is sharp in my veins. There's low conversation in a guttural foreign language, and it's only then that I realise I'm not hurt. I'm restrained, but no one has hit me, or so much as sworn as I struck out.

"Please." My voice is high-pitched and scared. I barely sound like myself. Even in years of the care-system, I've never been this afraid. "Ivan?"

It's a guess, but when your newly ex-boyfriend is furious with you, and the son of a Russian mafia boss, it's probably accurate.

No one replies.

"Please. Get Ivan." I'm trembling. My mind is whirling. I had an argument with Ivan yesterday, this has to be related?

My sister Hayley is going to be distraught. I can't die, I haven't lost my virginity yet. This can't be the end, I haven't even finished my degree. Is this what happened to my sister Taylor? Why have I been kidnapped? There's nothing special about me.

"Please let me go." There's still no response.

Then I'm pulled roughly to my feet. There's the sound of the door sliding open. My body jolts as the vehicle brakes.

Sunlight and a breath of wind touch my skin as I'm shoved from the van.

Someone ducks my head, sits me into a smooth leather seat, cuts whatever holds my hands, and pulls the blindfold away.

I blink at the brightness of the sudden light, dazed.

"Pakhan," a male voice says respectfully, and a car door thunks shut.

I jerk my head around, trying to get my bearings, but my eyes take a second to adjust. I'm in another vehicle, I realise as it moves. It's dimly lit, with leather seats, and darkened windows. A luxurious limo, with matte black and sparkling chrome.

For a moment, I think I'm on my own.

Then I see him.

A man. He has black hair that's scattered with silver-grey. His blue eyes are so deep they're almost navy, and his lashes are jet-black, and outrageously long for a man. They might make him look feminine, except for the shadow of stubble over his square jaw, and the bushy eyebrows that are low. His nose looks like it's been broken in several places, but his mouth is wide and his lips plush, even set as they are in a serious line.

Arrogantly sprawled opposite, he has one arm casually over the back of the seat, elegant fingers trailing down, and the other hand resting on his knee. Both are crossed with black ink. Tattoos.

His legs are apart, and he's wearing a charcoal suit with a pale-blue shirt that brings out the blue in his eyes. His shirt is open at the collar, the tie loosened, and the dip between his collarbones, the pronounced lump of his Adam's apple, and a few curls of black hair have an unfamiliar heat curling at the bottom of my abdomen.

He's gorgeous, and from his air of authority and the silver in his hair, seems older than me.

Old enough to be my dad, or someone else's. The harsh shape of his face and the dark-blue of his eyes echo in me.

Ivan. He reminds me of my ex-boyfriend, if he were more mature, hotter, and with the power and confidence of money and influence.

And that's when I know for sure I have to get out of here. My life is in danger.

I begin to shake.

I spin and grasp for the door handle. A mechanical sound of a lock clicking into place sounds, and nothing happens a split second before I yank. I pull it again and again, hoping, even as the limo picks up speed, panic rising in my chest and spilling out of my throat in a high-pitched whine of terror.

Spinning around, I'm just in time to see the man pocketing a remote control. He raises one sardonic eyebrow, and a shiver goes down my spine.

Russian accents, this man being deferentially called Pakhan, me upsetting Ivan. It's all too clear what's happening, and if what Ivan said is true, I'm toast.

Everything is on the table for getting away.

Anything.

It has to be. His men have just shown me the power of the element of surprise when they bundled me into a van from the street, and now being unpredictable is the only hope I have.

I have the life expectancy of a butterfly caught in a tornado.

Because this man isn't a random stranger. He's my ex-boyfriend's dad. And he's a feared Bratva mafia boss with a reputation for unhinged brutality.

2

FELIKS

She's beautiful.

I suppose it's not a surprise that my son shares my taste in women, but I didn't expect it, or his girlfriend to be so utterly gorgeous. She steals all my breath and my wits.

Her straight brown hair, pale-blue eyes, and heart-shaped face sound unremarkable when listed as attributes, but there's something very special about this girl.

She's dressed in a simple pair of cut-off jean shorts that show her long legs, and a plain white top. Her curves aren't on display, but the shape of her perfect handful breasts and the flare outwards from her waist to her hip is unbelievable.

The expression of shock on her face, and the shadow of fear, only make my cock throb all the more, because she examines me from head to toe.

It's an undeniable recognition as our eyes meet, for all that she's twenty years younger than me, and Ivan's girlfriend.

Something deep in my chest snarls *mine*.

I can't steal her from my son. That's immoral even by my standards, isn't it?

"You're Payton Love." An absurdly sweet name. It suits her.

She hesitates and presses her lips together. It only makes me more aware of how pretty she is. How vulnerable. She nods warily.

"I'm Feliks Rykov."

She shrinks back, her bottom lip trembling. She recognises my name.

That's good. I tell myself it's better she knows I'm a monster.

"My son Ivan is your boyfriend."

She lifts one shoulder, as though unwilling to confirm or deny.

"You're not seeing him anymore, and I need you out of the way." That emerges a little harsher than I intended, but the thought of Payton with Ivan now makes me sick in a personal sense, rather than merely because the combination of a sadistic man and an innocent woman is disastrous.

"Mr Rykov," she breathes, and my cock twitches. "Please, let me go."

"No." That's not going to happen.

I've been alone for decades. I don't think I've ever needed anyone. I've definitely never been in love, and I have no reason to care about this girl beyond offering safety. If she wants to leave and probably get herself tortured and killed by Ivan, what is it to me?

"Please." She's across the limo in a second, and falls to her knees before me. Her hair flows over her shoulders in a smooth waterfall, and now she's at my feet, I see the swell of her breasts, peeking out of her top. "I'll do anything. Just let me go."

"I'm not going to..." I begin to explain that I won't hurt

her, and this is for her safety, but she reaches for me, and it's all I can do to keep my mouth from falling open.

"I'll do whatever you want," she murmurs, brushing her palms onto my thighs, and I wonder whether she knows what a bad idea this is.

Speech is utterly outside of my capacity.

The conflict in me is painful, because this feels so right, and yet absolutely wrong. Having my son's girlfriend sliding her hands up my legs has electricity zapping down my spine and my palms itching to pull her close. To have her on my lap and to feel her soft-looking lips on mine.

On the other hand, I'm filled with revulsion that she's clearly doing this to try to escape. As a transaction, not because she wants me.

My cock doesn't know the difference, though, and is hardening as her hands get nearer to where I'm already dreaming of her touching.

But when she looks up into my face and I find her pale-blue irises dark, and her pupils blown, my pulse spikes.

She's half my age. She's probably in love with my son. She doesn't feel this connection between us because I'm imagining it.

That last one I can't make myself believe. She's doing this for the wrong reasons, yes, but she isn't repulsed by me.

Then her gaze flicks down to where I pocketed the key to the limo's central locking, and I get it.

"Tell me what you want me to do, sir." Her voice is pure sex, and she angles her chest forwards to give me a better—albeit still very limited—view of her tits.

"You seem more interested in what's in my pocket." It's meant as a warning, but it's too raspy. I'm getting aroused, exactly as she intends. Already, from her touch through my trousers, and not yet even on any part of significance.

She shakes her head as though she doesn't understand. "I'll do whatever you want if you'll let me go." Her hands creep further up my thighs, testing the muscle she finds there.

"Mmmhum." It's an effort not to smile. This girl is intent on getting away, not staying to discover whether my intentions are good or bad, and I respect that. "Reach for what you desire, Payton."

She reaches for my cock with one hand, and simultaneously for the car key with the other.

And as she does, I draw a knife from my jacket pocket. The blade flicks open with the push of a button, and I bring it to her neck, where her pulse beats fast.

Letting out a soft squeak of distress as she feels the cold steel, her hands still.

"Moya lisichka." The endearment slips out of my mouth instinctively. My little fox. She's smart and beautiful.

She has one hand on my half-hard cock, the car key in the other, and I have my knife to her throat.

We stare into each other's eyes, and I can see renewed fear there.

I don't think she's as experienced or as reckless as her actions suggest. She isn't showing me her exquisite body, or working my cock. She's as compelled as I am by this ridiculous situation, and brave. So brave.

Even unaware that I'd rather turn this knife against myself than actually hurt her, she's not moving.

She's my match. This girl who is young and innocent and forbidden, and whom I only intended to protect from my son.

Blood rushes to my cock as I look at her, and her little fingers rest on my growing erection. The spark between us is undeniable.

My hand is almost shaking. My heart is beating out of my chest. This feels like something.

Moreover, I feel. For a man who has spent his life not caring for anyone or anything, this is unheard of. It's exhilarating. It's terrifying.

I think she'll need protection from *me*.

3

PAYTON

He holds the knife steady at my throat even as his cock lengthens and thickens further under my hand.

My pulse flutters, and I'm more alive than I've ever felt.

My ex-boyfriend's dad is hard. Or rather, he's getting an erection as I watch, swelling in a way I knew happened to men—theoretically—but have never seen. I didn't imagine it would be so quick, or make my tummy flip with excitement.

It's not just how he's reacting to me, it's the power of it. Because I can see on his face the tussle of emotions, and almost... Fear?

He can't be afraid of me. I'm nothing.

But with his sensitive, hard cock clasped beneath my fingers, even with the fabric between us, I feel powerful. Like I'm in control, not him.

He has a knife to my throat, but his erection balances it out.

"You want to escape that much, lisichka?" I don't understand the Russian word, but this is hardly the moment to ask.

"Yes." I swallow and grip the key harder, but it's a lie.

Getting it was instinct, and touching him a rash way to get the upper hand, but now I'm staring up into this man's face, it feels like an excuse.

I want him to be strong enough to subdue every bratty tendency in me. To take me and make me his.

Is this a normal reaction to possible death?

I'm going to assume yes, since it's never happened to me before, I can't ask anyone, and I don't think the internet would help me even if I had my phone to search.

"So pretty," he murmurs, and presses the blade closer, his words rough with his Russian accent.

It's entirely messed up that he's hard, I'm trying to flee, and there's the threat of him slitting my throat, but I'm hot between my legs. I'm turning to molten lava.

I'm excited in a way I didn't realise was possible.

"Enough," he growls and in one smooth action he takes the knife from my neck and sheaths it, then plucks the key from my hand. Grabbing me underneath the arms, he lifts me as though I weigh nothing, dragging me over his thighs and setting me down next to him. Shifting away, he subtly rearranges his trousers, so his erection is less noticeable.

I say less, because something that big is like smuggling a baseball bat.

"As I was saying," he continues, as though the incident with the knife and his cock inches from my face didn't happen, and it's not quite a question. "You won't see my son again, and you're leaving London."

Dominant and dictatorial. I glare at him. It's a good thing I'm not in love with Ivan, because if I were, this would cause a major issue.

"How much do you know about what Ivan was doing?"

What's the right answer here? I'm not sure. Which answer will keep me alive?

"Why?" I'm proud of how I sound. Far stronger than I feel on the inside.

He pointedly doesn't look at me, and grits his teeth. In profile he's even more gorgeous, the stubble of his defined jaw dark. I wonder how it would be on my skin? Would it hurt, like sandpaper?

I think I might enjoy that.

"Because you're in danger. Ivan is..." But he trails off, not finishing the statement.

I curl into myself, because that sends a chill down my spine. Far too plausible. "Danger?"

"My son is in a lot of trouble, and is becoming..." He seems to choose his words carefully. "Erratic."

"The money," I say.

"What do you know about it?" he snaps, and turns towards me. Even sitting side by side—not touching now, he was careful to arrange that—he's so much taller than me that I have to tilt my head up to look at him.

"Ivan gave me gifts and he..." Why do I find it shameful?

Feliks waits patiently, dark eyes steady on my face as it heats. It's not great.

"He pursued me." It doesn't sound convincing, but it's true. "Ivan wanted me to be his girlfriend, and he gave me presents until I agreed."

I hate that I said yes.

"And you accepted," he points out with the sort of emotionless tone that smacks of judgement.

"I sell the stuff online and use the money to contribute to the household with my sister. She works really hard, and she wants me to succeed at university, so she won't let me work. The jewellery, tech, clothes, and accessories he showered me with paid for decent tea bags, fresh fruit, and cheese." It's pouring out, this truth. I can't stop it, and Feliks looks stunned. "I know the pressure gets a lot for her sometimes. Having food in the fridge to have a nice meal, and the occasional takeaway, has really helped."

I pause.

"Like really, really, made life better for Hayley and me. And there was enough that I could pay for a private investigator to locate our other sister, Taylor. He's made progress, too, discovering that she's probably with an exclusive ballet display group that tours the world. The PI just needs a bit more time to find where they are currently."

That's why I couldn't break up with Ivan, even though I wanted to. I couldn't because the Love sisters stick together.

All it cost was my dignity, self-respect, and as it turns out, possibly my life.

He nods, and there's a gleam in his dark eyes that I could swear is appreciation.

"And in return, you..." he says leadingly.

"I was his girlfriend." I tilt my chin up. I have nothing to be ashamed of. My neck is stiff, like my body is reluctant to be as bold about this as my mind is, but I'm ignoring that. "He got my attention."

And my god Ivan needs attention. He's impossible.

"And your body." Feliks' gaze drops slowly down, then back up, assessingly.

My skin prickles with heat under his gaze.

"Not that it's any of your business, but no." I'm pouting. "He had a kiss, and yesterday he said that wasn't enough, and that unless I..." I'm blushing.

"Fucked him," Feliks supplies matter-of-factly.

My throat goes dry. I glance out of the window, embarrassed. I don't recognise the buildings but we're near the outskirts of London now, judging by the peeks of fields and hills I can see on the horizon.

"Unless I did that, which would make me his proper girlfriend," I continue, gaze fixed outside. "I would have to give back everything he said I'd bought from him but not paid for. But they were gifts," I emphasise. "He said they were gifts."

"And his behaviour over the last few weeks?" Feliks doesn't even acknowledge my claim, and I can't tell from his tone whether it's because he believes me, or he doesn't. But there's something definite in his voice, as though either way, there's no question in his mind.

"He's been..." I hesitate as I think of Ivan's more manic than usual laugh, the way he's pushed me to go out with him and his friends when I said I didn't want to, and how he's been meaner, his grip on my arm painful when he held me. His jokes crueller, his expression harsher.

"Go on." Feliks nods seriously.

"I think..." I'm going to get Ivan into trouble, and for all he and I used each other—me to continue receiving the presents he gave me, and him for my untouchable vibe and attractive body—I don't want to cause trouble. "He might have been taking drugs?" I finish looking over at Feliks.

The corner of his mouth twitches up. "If that was all, you wouldn't be here, lisichka."

"What did he do?" My tummy flips. I'm not actually sure I want to know.

"You seem to have been a decoy for his other activities."

What? What does that mean? As I open my mouth to ask, the limo takes a sharp turn, and we pull up to high metal chain-link gates that swing open for us. There's concrete, and huge, curved-roof buildings.

An airfield.

"Why are we here?" I can see what an airfield is usually for, but this makes no sense. Feliks' gaze locks onto a plane with a jagged black emblem on the tail, a set of steps out the side, and a couple with suitcases approaching from a car.

"To kill some people," he growls.

What?!

4

FELIKS

"No!" Payton protests. "No, surely that's—"

I don't stop to listen.

"Stay here," I snarl and as the limo halts, I push to my feet and I'm out and striding towards my private jet.

"Yes, but will there be Champagne?" the woman is saying to my pilot as I approach. My Beckenham men who dragged Payton from the street have just arrived ahead of me, but this is clearly something they weren't prepared to deal with, and they look baffled.

"I think we can cope with Cava," the man next to her says reassuringly, but with a note of question.

"But this is our dream wedding trip!" she replies hysterically. "Everything has to be the very best, and Cava isn't…"

My pilot's gaze bounces between the woman and me. "Pakhan," he begins.

I draw the revolver from under my jacket. "Nyet."

The couple turn and the woman screams, though I'm not pointing the gun at her.

"What the fuck do you think you're doing?" I demand.

Out of the corner of my eye, I spot a small figure creep out of the limo, and I exhale with exasperation.

"Payton," I snarl, and she freezes.

Still trying to escape. So brave, and sweet, and naive as a baby bird. I was so distracted by this gavno, I forgot to lock the door behind me.

"Encircle her, but do not touch her," I mutter to the nearest of my men, and they slip off to do my bidding.

"Do not think of running, Payton. You will have blood on your hands if I have to kill him," I nod at the pilot, "to chase after you."

She makes a cute sound of frustration.

The woman begins to sob, and throws herself into her partner's arms. He looks as though he might vomit, but does a good job restraining both her, and his breakfast.

"This isn't what it seems," the pilot says, like a fucking cliché.

"It never is." I'm weary of this.

I crook one finger, beckoning Payton to me. Shooting wary looks at my men who now surround her, she walks over in jerky motions, her head bowed.

As soon as she's near enough, I grab her little hand and drag her to my side. It's delicate in my big paw, and I try not to notice it too much, or squeeze her too tight, as I lace our fingers together.

I'm soothed by having her close.

"In what way is this not you taking my private jet—which I pay you to have at my disposal anytime—without my permission?" I ask the pilot.

"It's not!" the woman screeches. "This is my private jet to take me to my tropical wedding!"

I rub my jaw thoughtfully, and raise my eyebrows at the pilot.

"Tropical wedding," I repeat, in a voice that any sane person would recognise as pure menace.

The man beside her is obviously either stupid or insane, as not only is he presumably this screech-owl's fiancé, he doesn't understand the danger, or that I wasn't asking a question. I was inviting my pilot to ensure this was fixed immediately.

"Now, look here," the man begins, standing up straighter.

He's dwarfed by my six-foot-five frame. I glance at him, and to his credit, he doesn't back down.

"I paid for a luxury beach wedding elopement and two-week honeymoon on an exclusive island." His voice wobbles. "And I promised that to my fiancée, and so if you could…"

Turning the gun on him has his wife-to-be screaming again.

I think he just realised he's really at risk, because I'm feeling murderous, my lip curling as I listen to this bullshit when I should be getting Payton Love onto this plane, and away from London, safe, then going after the monster with my name and half my DNA.

"Let us go…" he finishes pathetically.

Pizdets. This is enough.

"I do not run a FUCKING TRAVEL COMPANY!" I roar.

The pilot cringes, which is logical. If it weren't for the fact he knows how to fly my private plane, and pilots are difficult to get at late notice and I want Payton out of the way while I deal with Ivan, he'd be dead already.

"My name is Feliks Rykov. You might know me," I say more calmly. "As the head of the Beckenham Bratva." I let my Russian accent bleed through a little more.

Yes. They recognise that name. My reputation for being unhinged has been carefully cultivated with the deaths of those who deserve it, and the creation of weapons that are as genius as they are terrifying. Their horror shows, except for Payton, whose brows knit with confusion.

"Feliks." There's a gentle tug at my hand, I glance down at Payton's upturned face. Her enormous eyes are trusting.

No one has trusted me for years. Decades. Ever.

"They just want to get married," she says in a small voice, and fuck, but she has no sense of self-preservation, what makes her think she should intervene in a deadly situation?

Except, she's correct. There's one force on earth that can calm me, and it's this girl. Slowly, I lower my weapon, and holster it, focusing on her little hand in mine. Trying to be a good enough man for her.

"Why are you taking them on a fucking wedding trip?" I ask the pilot.

"I thought you knew, Pakhan," he stammers, sweat having beaded at his temple, and I go cold. Because of course. I should have known.

My son.

"Ivan told me it was at your instruction."

"Yes, that's the name of the customer service agent who promised me champagne on the flight!" the woman exclaims.

"What *exactly* did my son sell you?" I demand.

"A full wedding package," the man says.

Mudak. Ivan needed money so badly that he sold luxury wedding packages to my island. Camden really did have his balls in a vice.

"Well, he didn't have the right to sell you anything, and she's taking this plane." I nod at Payton.

I've wasted enough time on this already. I need this distracting girl out of the way, then I can take out my bloody anger on the person who deserves it. Ivan.

"I'm not having a stranger on my exclusive flight!" the woman objects, loudly. Her voice is a cross between nails on a chalkboard and the sound of a six-year-old playing the violin.

"No," I say. "You're not getting on that plane, because, as I've mentioned before, it belongs to me."

"I'll report you to the—"

"Please darling," her husband-to-be begs.

I've had enough of this shit. My hand twitches for my gun but Payton's interlocked fingers tightening on mine stop me. I look down at her.

"It's her wedding."

Oh fuck why do I have to have a weak spot the size of the Atlantic for this girl?

She's your son's girlfriend, I remind myself.

She won't be for long, a voice reminds me. As soon as Payton is safely on that plane, I will go to kill my offspring.

The things a father has to do.

"You." I point at the pilot. "If this plane isn't in the air in five minutes your head will be all over the tarmac."

I turn to the wedding couple. "I'll refund whatever you paid, and if you go to Beckenham Court House in my car now, you can get married. Which I assume is the most important part of this trip." I arch an eyebrow.

"But what about the floral pergola on the beach—" the woman protests.

"Consider yourself lucky to be alive," I mutter and walk away, dragging Payton behind me. I take the stairs up to the jet two at a time, and she has to run to keep up.

"Get your hands off me!" comes a screechy voice from

below as we enter the plane, so I assume my men have done their jobs and are getting rid of the results of Ivan's little travel-agent hobby.

I refocus fully on Payton Love.

She's sharing her glances between me and the luxurious aircraft as I pull her further inside to large, comfortable leather seats and... Oh the irony, there's a bottle of bubbly on ice. Champagne.

I guide Payton to a seat, and before I've thought better of it, sit next to her.

"Pakhan." The senior flight attendant approaches me, head bowed.

I spend a lot of time at my secondary residence, a private tropical island I bought almost twenty-five years ago, when I made my first obscene amount of money with a new weapon that became vital to every country that could afford it. So the jet's staff are familiar with me.

They also know that I can be unpredictable, and potentially deadly. I once had to take a dead body on a flight and this stewardess hasn't been comfortable with me since.

"We're ready to go now." She doesn't meet my gaze.

This is my cue to leave.

I feel the words. They're just behind my tongue.

"What's going to happen?" Payton asks in a small voice.

The plan was to ditch Payton in a safe house an hour away in Scotland to keep her out of the way until I'd dealt with her boyfriend. My island, on the other hand is much further across the ocean, then a boat trip that takes a couple more hours.

"Ivan will discover that I'm onto him and his scam of selling wedding packages to fund Camden's blackmail, as well as the 'hobby' that got him into this trouble. If he's desperate for money, or thinks he has nothing to lose, he'll come after you."

She creases her brow in confusion.

"It seems everything is in place for a trip to my private island, so you can go there. I think you'll enjoy the weather there more than where I was going to send you in Scotland."

I should explain fully and then leave. But Payton's lip wobbles.

"Can I have my phone?" she asks in a small voice. "There's someone I need to talk to."

"Ivan?" I ask with dangerous calm, fury bubbling to the surface.

"No," she whispers.

I can't risk it anyway. Who knows what software Ivan has put on her phone. I can't drag my gaze from Payton, never mind walk away. She's innocent. Pretty. Not even half my age.

She's not mine. But she feels like she's mine, and the thought of deserting her to go to my son as though that piece of shit matters makes me crazy.

Because as it turns out, she is the only one that matters.

Moya lisichka. In less than an hour, this girl has found her way into my heart, triggering a protective instinct that has been dormant for forty-four years. She's the perfect combination of brave and sweet and vulnerable.

I have to prevent any more fuck-ups, I tell myself. It's not because I'm falling for her. It's not because I can't stand to spend another minute without her.

I'll return to London tomorrow, and do what I have to, and no parent ever should. In the meantime, I'll look after Payton, help her get settled into the island and explain she'll be alone for some days until I've dealt with Ivan. What's the harm of letting him live, and keeping my soul a bit cleaner, for one more day?

"You won't need your phone. I'll be your social secretary," I say dryly.

"My what?" she says, gaping.

Picking up the Champagne bottle from the silver cooler, I rip off the foil, and pop the cork. Nodding to the stewardess, I pour a flute and pass it to Payton, who blinks, confused, but accepts the glass. "We're going to the beach."

For a destination wedding.

5

PAYTON

I've never been on a plane. I haven't drunk Champagne before. I've never seen anyone thinking about shooting a person. And most important of the fresh experiences, the way I feel with Feliks' eyes on me is different to anything else.

The bubbles go straight to my head. Probably I shouldn't accept anything from my captor, but he's drinking too, and for some bizarre reason, I trust Feliks.

He could have taken advantage of me, he could have hurt me, he could have just left me to be a victim of whatever Ivan is doing, but he hasn't.

He's scary, but something about him calls to a wisp of darkness I wasn't aware was inside me.

The flight attendant gives me a safety talk, impressing on me the importance of the seatbelt and pointing out the exits, as well as alarming things like what to do if the cabin depressurises. But I'm distracted by Feliks making a phone call.

"Find and secure Ivan," he says, taking a slug of Champagne, then slides his gaze over to me and our eyes meet. He scowls, switches to Russian, and rattles off more instructions, not even pretending to listen to the safety briefing.

He continues on the phone all the way until the plane starts moving, when he shuts it off. Then before I know it, I'm mesmerised by watching out of the window as we pick up speed. I'm pushed back in my seat, and then my tummy flips as we tilt upwards and then soar smoothly up, the ground dropping away.

Everything below shrinks as we fly into the air. The runway is quickly out of sight, then there's a patchwork of fields and little houses, tiny toy cars on ribbons of grey. It's a new perspective. I don't think I've seen a take-off on television, but even if I had, it wouldn't compare to the weight of my body being swooped up with the aircraft and the buzzing in my veins.

A wisp flies past the window, then another. Then we break up into clouds, and I do something ridiculous, like gasp. There's pressure bubbling out of my ears, then they do this weird clicking pop, and I'm fine again. Outside, it's pure white, as though the plane is wrapped in cotton wool.

I blink.

I knew clouds weren't solid. But even so, I'm amazed by cutting into the white blanket hanging over London.

Unreal.

I'm about to turn away, when as quickly as we plunged into the cloud, we break out, the sun blinding. We're above the white fluff that looks soft and firm, as though you could bounce on it, the most comfortable mattress in the world.

"Flying for the first time is special." Feliks' voice snaps me out of my obsession.

"How did you know?" I ask, though it's obvious, I

suppose. How could I have flown anywhere before? With what money?

I try to sit up and be cool. Maybe even summon a bit of anxiety over the fact I don't have my phone, don't know where we're going, and have been kidnapped by my ex-boyfriend's father who nearly killed someone earlier.

He gazes at me for a long moment, his expression unreadable, then at last murmurs, "You have stars in your eyes."

"Sorry," I say reflexively.

His brows lower. "Never apologise for enjoying something that doesn't hurt anyone else."

Oh. Oh, that's... Okay. I guess I often feel guilty about lots of things. Selling the gifts from Ivan for starters, or anytime I'm reading instead of studying, because I know how important it is to Hayley that I get a good education.

I glance out of the window again, and the sunshine above the clouds really is amazing. It's been there all along, even when I've been on the ground, in the drizzly London rain.

All it took was for Feliks to bring me up here.

"Where are we going?" I look back at Feliks, because compelling as the view is, he has my curiosity piqued more.

"My private island, south-west of London."

Another infuriatingly vague answer. "And how long will it take for us to get there?"

"Long enough for you to have your fill of cloud-watching, and have a nap as well. And there are films you can watch if you get bored of looking out of the window."

My excitement must show on my face, because Feliks laughs indulgently. He shows me the personal mini-screen that pops out of the arm rest, and gives me headphones for it.

There are recent releases, and games, and this massive leather seat is actually really comfy. I alternate watching a romcom I wanted to see at the cinema but couldn't afford to, and the view from the window. By the time the cloud clears to reveal the ground again, we're over the ocean, and it's endless blue.

Feliks sits beside me, his arm draped onto our shared armrest and though there's plenty of space, I don't know why, but I have to put my arm there too. So we're almost brushing sleeves.

I lose track of time, because the flight attendant brings drinks—I don't have any more Champagne, but I had enough to make me light-headed and not as worried as I should be—and snacks, and what turns out to be a seven course lunch that we eat in comfortable silence, Feliks working on a laptop, and me watching a second film.

The stewardess shows me to a toilet with a full shower that's bigger than the one in Hayley's and my rented house, and a bedroom. But I'm not tired. So it's only after that, when I really can't eat any more food, and I've tried all the games that interest me and read the descriptions of half the movies available, that I begin to get bored, curious, and a bit anxious.

"Why have you kidnapped me?" I take the earbuds out and ask my captor.

Feliks sighs and puts his laptop away, turning to look at me. "I told you."

That Ivan was dangerous, and a threat. I chew my lower lip as I think. "But you said you were going to go and sort out Ivan?"

I don't say murder, even though I'm pretty sure that's what he meant.

Feliks grits his teeth, and I wait.

Nope. Nothing.

"Truth or dare," I say on impulse. The Champagne really must have gone to my head.

"You really are twenty-one, aren't you?" he drawls, leaning back in his seat and regarding me with a wry expression.

"Yes," I reply promptly. "I'll take that as your first truth question, now I get one. How old are you?"

He has more grey than black in his hair, and he's Ivan's dad, so obviously he's older than me, but I want to know how much.

He huffs with laughter. "Twice your age plus twice the number of babies I accidentally fathered when I was your age."

"Uh..." He has Ivan, but does he have any other children? And is that jealousy of whoever he loved when I was a baby? Wild. I'm losing my mind.

"Forty-four." He has a wry tilt to his mouth.

Oooohhh. I know it's totally inappropriate, but I find it hot that he's so much older than me. But given I'm still coping with my terrible response to being kidnapped, manhandled, and seeing him pull a gun on a person who was very annoying, I guess I shouldn't be surprised.

"Why did you hire a PI to look for your sister?" he asks after a second.

"We're not doing dares?" I reply.

He raises one totally unimpressed eyebrow.

"No, no, okay." I force my breath out between my teeth. I asked for this. "Taylor disappeared from London, well, from somewhere in Russia, we think—"

"She *what*?" Feliks' expression has gone hawk-like.

"She's a ballerina. We were all in care after our mother

died, and she was sent to this awesome ballet school in London," I explain.

"In Richmond, yes." Feliks nods for me to continue.

"She said she had an even better opportunity, and then she just stopped communicating." I shrug. The hurt is familiar now, but I still miss Taylor. "Hayley—my other sister, she's the eldest—tried to get the police involved, and she searches for Taylor herself. But it…"

I shake my head, unable to explain how the police didn't take our concerns seriously until it was too late, and the trail had gone totally cold.

"Girls from care are an easy target, and not high priority," he grits out.

"That's about it." My fingertips trace the leather of our joint armrest, and for a second, he shifts, and the backs of our hands touch. A brief moment, there and gone, that sends electricity down my spine. But when I look up into Feliks' face there's nothing but compassion.

"All my life, I've been the baby, the one cared for and protected by my sisters." I don't know why I explain more. He didn't ask, but I'm compelled to tell him. "I've wanted to stand on my own feet, to contribute, and Ivan's gifts that I could sell to help without having to spend hours more working was too good to say no to. Ivan was the one who pursued me and gave me gifts, not the other way around."

Feliks nods. "You said the PI found her ballet troupe?"

"Maybe. That's why I kept on with Ivan even when…" I didn't want to be his girlfriend anymore, even before we argued about the "gifts". But how could I stop?

"He made you uncomfortable," Feliks fills in after a moment of silence from me.

"Yes. But it's a long shot." I've kind of given up hope of finding Taylor, but that doesn't mean I'm going to stop.

There's a sad silence, and maybe talking about Taylor has given me the feeling I've nothing left to lose, as I turn in my seat, and square my shoulders, and ask what's been bothering me since the limo ride.

"You implied that Ivan was involved in something worse than drugs. What's going on?"

6

FELIKS

The pain of hearing Payton mention Ivan—my biggest mistake and regret—is enough to make me want to request a dare instead of truth, and hope it's to jump out of the plane.

"Do not ask questions you don't want to know the answer to, Payton," I reply, and I pray she takes my advice.

"Was it a mafia betrayal?" she insists. "He said something about Camden?"

I bark with laughter, though it's not funny.

"No. I wish it were so simple."

She curls her feet up into the large leather seat so she can look more easily across at me, but keeps her seat belt on. Such a good girl.

I'd love to corrupt her, starting with dragging her into my lap and fucking her right here.

Instead, I'm going to tell her the truth.

"Beckenham's main business is in high-tech solutions for physical security—the sort of things that people don't want us to be able to do—but I do dabble in online surveillance as well, since that's often related. And it was during a routine check that I discovered Ivan and his friends have tastes that even an immoral bastard like me doesn't condone."

She looks confused, poor innocent.

"He likes to torture those who don't want or deserve it." Which is something I could live with if it were confined to mafia business or consensual adults. I've inflicted plenty of suffering in my time, for the sake of ensuring Beckenham is respected and feared. But it wasn't that. There were a lot of recordings, and they were clearly for my son's sick entertainment. "People. And animals, too."

The dawning horror on her face is grim. I wish I could save her from this, but at least she hasn't seen the video footage that I have.

"It turns out Camden discovered before I did, and were blackmailing him. I think that's why he was so keen to have you as a girlfriend. You were a plausible cover that he had a pretty girlfriend, and so I wouldn't look for any other interest he might have." It worked, for a while, and I'm torn as to be more angry that Ivan had Payton or that he duped me. "And you were a reason he needed the money he was actually spending on trafficking his true interests, and paying Camden for their silence."

Her mouth falls open in shock, then I can see every emotion flitting across her face as she lines up all the evidence in her mind. Disbelief, understanding, dismay. Hurt.

"He wanted a girlfriend that wasn't really a girlfriend." She says it like it makes horrible sense. "To cover his tracks."

I nod grimly. "It seems Camden were raising the stakes and the cost week by week. But he couldn't afford for me to find out."

"Why not?"

My mouth sets in a harsh line. "My silence cannot be bought. Ivan knew he would pay in blood."

"Oh." Her eyes go wide. "His expenses kept on rising, so he was looking to cut costs. Not having a girlfriend anymore, clawing back some of the money, and maybe..."

Neither of us complete that thought. If he was paying so much to Camden that he needed her gifts returned, he might also have decided to hunt for victims closer to home. Payton would be an obvious person to take out his sadistic anger on.

She fidgets and looks away, picking up and putting down her half-finished orange juice that she asked for after the glass of Champagne.

"That's enough high-drama," I say. She's safe, at least for now. "Your turn. Truth or dare?"

Payton's eyes fill with worry, and she hesitates before replying, "Truth."

Pity. I'd have liked to dare her to kiss me. That could have distracted us both very effectively.

"Tell me something that you love doing,"

She blinks, taken aback, then replies, "Swimming."

I grin. She's going to adore the beach house. "Where do you swim?"

"At an outdoor pool in Richmond."

I nod slowly. "There's one in Beckenham too, and a big park."

I don't mention the clear blue waters around the island I'm taking her to. I'd rather enjoy her surprise as she sees it for the first time.

"Is that it?" she asks when I don't follow up.

"Da." And I brace myself, because I sense that my respite will be short. "You can ask another question."

"Where's Ivan's mother?" she says immediately.

My heart sinks. This whole conversation doesn't cast me in a flattering light, and I've discovered that it matters very much what she thinks of me.

"And what happened that he ended up..." she trails off, unsure how to say the awkward thing.

A monster. My son is a monster, even amongst mafia bosses.

"He turned up on my doorstep, aged eighteen," I reply. "His mother had told him my name, after years of keeping it a secret from him, and he came to find me."

I'd stared into the face of my younger self that day. I hadn't even asked for a paternity test. Ivan had insisted, so I'd bled onto the sample and sent it off. But the result was never in question.

He had my chin, and eyes, and all the arrogance I'd had when I was eighteen, but without any of the natural ability for mafia work. None of the instincts, and definitely zero skills.

The blood lust though. The cold, vicious streak. He had that, and I tried to tell myself at the time that it was normal.

"I didn't know what to do with him," I admit. "I insisted he go to university because I thought it would give him an opportunity to grow up. Mature. And maybe be useful to Beckenham afterwards."

"He was studying computer science," she says, evidently still processing all this, since I already know that.

I nod. "There isn't a degree in mafia management, unfortunately."

That makes her snort with laughter, but her smile dies quickly. "Did you not know about Ivan, then? If he just turned up, it was good of you to accept him."

Such a sweet girl. She's trying to make me less culpable.

"I paid the money due and never saw him. I regret that.

I was a bad father." Guilt grabs me by the throat. If I had kids now, I'd be in their lives.

I can't help my gaze dragging over Payton's body, imagining her pregnant with a baby we both desperately wanted, and would dote on.

"Why did you have a child at all?"

"I didn't mean to. But no method of contraception is perfect, and by the time his mother told me, we were having a child whether we liked it or not. And I didn't like it." I'd speculated about whether it had been accidental, especially because Ivan's mother had informed me of the pregnancy at three months. But eventually I'd decided that the answer was not to take any more risks, and I haven't since. My hand might not be as good as a cunt, but it can't get into trouble. "I was far too young, involved in building a territory in London. I had experienced losing my family when a small Russian Bratva killed them and took me in when I was sixteen. My father had been dealing drugs, and tried to double-cross the Pakhan—that's the name of the head of a Bratva, it means eldest brother—and found to his cost that it is a bad idea."

I twist my mouth wryly. "I had only just destroyed that group from the inside out, like an apple rotting from the core. I wasn't keen to experience any of that again."

"I'm sorry for your loss." There's distress in her voice.

"Thank you," I reply mechanically. "It was a long time ago."

"So you've given up on family? I can't imagine life without my sisters." She stares at her hands in her lap, obviously thinking of them. "You don't ever want children?"

"No, it's..." I don't know how to answer her, but that's wrong.

She turns back, waiting for my answer as though it's important to her. And it is to me too.

"The truth is so much more complicated. Twenty-year-old mafia bosses shouldn't have children." I raise my eyebrows. "Ivan hasn't had loss to make him realise the consequences of his actions." I'm known for having no heart, but I have limits. Ivan could have been me, if I'd been coddled and indulged. Just vicious impulses with no empathy. "His mother raised a savage dog with my genetics, and I have to put it down."

"I understand." She tilts her chin up.

"But if I had children now..." I let the thought linger, careful to keep my gaze on her face, however much I want it to drop to her breasts, her waist, her hips. That place between her legs that after more than twenty years, I finally have an insatiable urge to taste. She was born the same year as Ivan, and it's as though I've been waiting all this time for her.

"I'm ready now," I say softly, and it's true. "I'm forty-four. A lot has changed in twenty-one years, and I like the idea of stopping thinking of myself and my own achievements, and caring for a family." The itch of discontent and loneliness has been growing for a long time now.

"Perhaps it took that long to heal from your family being murdered," she whispers back.

My throat clogs, and I dip my head. "Yes," I manage to get out, a bit strangled. "I'm powerful now. I could protect those I love."

The roar of the jet's engines is loud, but the thud of my heart as I look at Payton is deafening.

"What else do you like to do, aside from swim?" I ask eventually. And she accepts my change of subject gracefully, replying that she likes to read. We don't need to exchange truth questions after that, because she's telling me about the fantasy romances she enjoys, and then the true crime podcasts. She tells me her favourite unsolved cases, and my job is finally an advantage because I can explain how an "impossible" crime could have been carried out—and possibly was with one of my products—and we continue talking for hours, except to accept food and refreshment from the cabin crew.

It's only when I check my watch and see we're only half an hour from landing, and I notice her wince again, as though something hurts, and my heart lurches.

"What is it?" I demand.

"Pain," she gasps, holding her fingers to her ears. Her face creases in discomfort, and panic, red and hot and sharp, floods my veins.

7

PAYTON

The pressure has been building up for a few minutes in my ears, but it's harsher suddenly. It's horrible. I'm a wuss about pain, admittedly, but why...? Tears threaten behind my eyes, and I slump in my chair, rubbing my temples.

"Payton, listen to me." Feliks is there, cupping my jaw with his palm, and speaking low and urgently. "It's okay. Your ears aren't equalising. Swallow for me."

"What?" I can't think past how he's touching me. His hand is warm, and his fingertips are a little rough.

He makes a frustrated sound, then the next second he has a bottle of water, the lid crunching as he twists it efficiently off. "Here. Drink."

I take it from him dubiously, and when I go to drink, he tips up my chin as I do.

And my god. As the first mouthful goes down my throat, something eases in my ears, the pain lessening.

"That's it," he croons, and he's brushing my hair away from my face with one long finger, and watching me carefully. "Better?"

Drinking again, it sort of pops this time, and I had no

idea it was so nice for my head to feel almost normal, and not as though it's about to explode.

The starkly tattooed hand that brushed hair from my eyes continues stroking down to the nape of my neck, and despite everything, it feels good.

I struggle not to lean into his touch as he strokes my hair again, then again.

I can't get over how lovely it is to be held near his big chest, to have his big hand on my hair. Hayley and I hug, of course, but it doesn't feel anything like this. It's not like being protected, a huge wall of man between you and the world.

"When you've flown dozens of times, you'll laugh about this," he says in a deep, rumbling voice.

"Hardly likely." When am I going to be able to afford to take a plane again? This might be a bougie kidnapping, but afterwards I'll be straight back to counting pennies and student loans. Especially with Ivan gone.

Well. Unless I'm dead.

"What happened to me?" I ask to cover my increasing embarrassment and a squirmy feeling of heat between my legs and excitement in my tummy.

"It was the pressure difference between the air inside your ears." He traces his thumb over that part, giving the sensitive lobe a little squeeze, and I have to bite back a moan. "And the pressure of the air outside. And as we descend, the pressure is higher, and your ears hurt because that air is pushing to get inside." He smooths his hand down my hair again then gently tightens his grip, tugging at pleasure sensors I didn't know I had on my scalp. "Swallowing helps get air into that tiny space in your ear, so the air is the same inside and out."

"Oh." I feel so stupid.

Shifting to his seat beside mine, he brings my head to rest on his shoulder as we land. I don't even see the ground hurtling towards us, because I'm breathing in the salt water and citrus scent of Feliks and despite the discomfort in my ears, I like him stroking my hair.

A lot.

When the plane has landed and Feliks leads me out onto a set of metal stairs, we're met by a wall of warmth unlike anything I've felt. It's fragrant and dense. But I don't get to marvel at it for long, because we're in another car—a solid SUV this time—within a second, and when I ask Feliks about passports, he just rolls his eyes and says that doesn't apply to him or his guests.

He has an abrupt conversation during the car ride, all in Russian, but I recognise the word "Ivan", and Feliks looks grave when it's finished.

"My men can't find him," he explains to me when I give him an enquiring look.

Which is concerning, but by the time we're on a freaking boat, I can't hold onto the worry. This is luxury on a different level to anything I've ever seen. When Hayley and I arrived in London, we went to Buckingham Palace, and that was one thing. It was gold and floral fabrics. This though, isn't obvious. It's the sort of comfort that's new, and the finest of everything. The most expensive version.

He points out the island when it's a speck in the distance and we watch as we draw closer, it's an emerald-green and yellow gemstone in a gleaming blue sea and bright sky. And that is even more amazing than the boat and the jet.

A private island, complete with lush jungle and sparkling sandy beaches.

The house Feliks leads me into is surprising. After the

expensive vibes of his plane and boat, it's quite simple. Tiled floors, wooden furniture, bare wood beams. It's deliciously cool compared to the heat outside though.

He shrugs off his suit jacket in the kitchen, and lays it over the back of a chair before removing his tie and rolling up his shirt sleeves. I watch, entranced, as he reveals tanned forearms covered in dark hair. Strong. Bulky.

On his right arm there are tattoos, all black outline drawings perfectly slotted in but not touching. As though his whole body is a carefully crafted set of artworks that were designed to fit together. I spy a skull, what looks like a drone, and a boat, but mostly I can't make them out.

His left has a long snake that coils around his bicep, the head on his shoulder, staring up into Feliks' face.

But what really catches my attention are his wrists. His are square and unbreakable looking, and black tattoo lines fall over a scatter of black hair. It doesn't sound like the best part of a man's body, but the pure masculinity of him makes me squirmy. His wrists, his big hands, and the point where his shirt hides the firmness of his arm muscles. Swoon.

He notices me watching him, and smirks. I turn, blushing. He's just so hot.

"So, kidnapper, what are we going to do now?" I try to cover my embarrassment.

"What does anyone do when they get to a beach house?"

I jump, because his voice is close, and out of the corner of my eye I see him holding out a can of fizzy drink for me.

It's cold from the fridge, and lets out a satisfying tishh when I open it.

The heat is what's making me warm and liquid everywhere. Not him. Surely? "They go to the beach."

I sneak a look at Feliks as he takes a long sip from his own can.

It's a soft drink, same as he gave me, but somehow, he makes it sexy. The bob of his Adam's apple as he drinks, and the way his stubble blends into his neck. I want to see more of him. That's definitely wrong. Taboo. He's my ex-boyfriend's father, old enough to be my dad, and he's kidnapped me.

But the anger doesn't surface beyond a worry about Hayley being out of her mind from not knowing where I am.

"Come on." He hovers his hand at the small of my back and shepherds me to hinge sliding doors that he opens with a key. Then we're out on decking that ends on the sand. On the beach itself, and I gasp.

It's as perfect as those images you see on social media. The sky bluer than I could believe possible, the water almost still and utterly clear, turquoise-blue. The sand is creamy-yellow, and incredibly fine. Palm trees edge the beach, and it curves out of sight.

"Oh..." I knew I liked water. I knew I loved the sea, although I've been precious few times. But this? This is next level.

Every cell in my body has relaxed, like I'm home.

"Beautiful."

When I tear my eyes from greedily taking in the view, I find that he's watching me, not the sea. His eyes dip to my mouth with slow deliberateness that heats me more than the sun, and a delicious shiver goes up and down my spine.

He turns back to towards the ocean.

"Whenever I've been away for a while, I begin to wonder if I made a mistake buying this island," he says, conversationally. "And then I visit, and I realise I'd have paid more. Twice, or three times as much, ten times, and it still would be cheap for the feeling of peace I have here. Nowhere on earth is as good."

"Yeah," I breathe. "I get that."

I feel that way too. In this place, with this man by my side, there's a sense of safety. I've never felt truly safe. Yes, I'm the baby of the Love sisters, and Hayley protected me. Taylor too. But we were all kids, and we never had adults to look after us, and in particular, not a dad. No one who loved us, except each other.

And the weird thing is, this big, burly man is obviously not my dad. But as my captor, he's responsible for me, and there's the weirdest comfort in that. And he's looking at me as though he's obsessed. And I like it.

"I think you do," he murmurs. "Want to swim?"

I hesitate. "Can I phone my sister first?" By my guess, Hayley will be finishing work around now, and she'll be distressed when she gets home and I'm not there.

He sighs deeply. "That would be very inconvenient for me, and risky for you."

That's a softened stance from him. Something to work on. "Well. Do you have a spare swimsuit I could use?"

"There aren't any spares, no. I've never brought anyone else here."

I blink. "Seriously?"

Skinny dipping. It's my first thought. With Feliks. The idea is surprisingly appealing, and in combination with the fact that he says I'm the first woman to be here?

That squishy, warm sensation returns to my tummy. Butterflies, but caffeinated and wearing padded suits.

"But I made arrangements," he continues, "and there will be what you need."

He heads back into the house without another word,

and I'm left trotting after him like a baffled pony. I follow the sounds of his movement until I reach a door, and peek around it.

And my heart slams into my ribs. He's standing in a large room with an enormous bed. He's stripping off his shirt, and I get a flash of his chest, covered in tattoos and rippling with hard muscle, before I duck out.

"Sorry!" I squeal. "I thought..."

I press my back to the wall like I had a narrow escape and might still be in danger from proximity to a man that sexy taking his clothes off.

A rumbling laugh comes from Feliks.

There's the sound of fabric on skin, the clink of a belt, and the crackle of a zip. I imagine, fuzzily given my inexperience, what he's doing and how it would look. Feliks, my ex-boyfriend's dad, naked.

8

PAYTON

"It's safe now, lisichka, you can come in," he calls after a minute.

Nervously, I peer around the doorway, and nearly scream again.

Because, yes, technically he's right. But he is casually doing up the laces at the front of a pair of board shorts and I am not prepared for the sight of him half naked.

He's lined with tattoos, all over his chest and upper arms. Beneath the black ink and hair, he's in amazing shape. His biceps are defined, and his shoulders are wide so his whole chest tapers to his waist. His belly is flat, with a six pack, and his hips topped with a "V" of muscle.

He's so different to me. His hair, for one. I've never thought about a man's nipples, but his penny-like disks surrounded by scattered dark hair make me want to run my lips over it.

And the way a teasing trail of hair leads down to the line of his shorts, low on his hips....

Ooof.

"There's a suitcase of clothes for you." He nods at the space under a window.

"Thanks," I say, still struggling to look away from him.

I pause before I open the case, and I'm glad I'm braced, because the first thing I see is a white dress. A stunning, white dress that's floor length, and obviously intended for a bride.

"Uh, I think there's been a mistake." I finger the dress, and can't help but lift it out and hold it in front of me, turning to Feliks.

He pauses. "A misunderstanding, perhaps. But it will fit, yes? Not a mistake."

My brow furrows in confusion.

"I'll leave you to get changed to swim," he continues, barely looking up. "I'll be in the lounge."

Under the dress, I find shorts, T-shirts, white cotton knickers, and sundresses that are perfect for throwing on over a bikini. It's all tagged and pristine, and there's even some toiletries.

And two bikinis, but no one-piece that I'd usually go for swimming. I dither a bit, before choosing the blue bikini with tie sides. I'm self-conscious as I check myself in the mirrored doors of the wardrobe. I swim a lot, so this should be normal, but the thought of Feliks' eyes on me is different.

I wrap a soft turquoise sarong around me, leave my clothes in a neat pile, and go out to find Feliks.

"Did you put on sunscreen?" he asks without looking up when I enter the lounge. He's reclined on a sofa with a laptop before him.

"No." I scuff my bare feet. I hadn't even thought of that, but obviously I need it, or I'll burn to a crisp within minutes. Unlike Feliks, who is gorgeously tanned.

"Well." He gestures at the table, where there's a bottle

of sunscreen. Then he glances up, and the impact of him seeing me partly revealed under the sarong is gratifying to say the least. His pupils dilate as he takes me in.

I bite my lip. *Focus on the important points, not the way he makes you feel, Payton. He kidnapped you.*

"Unless you need Daddy to help you," he says, and I think it's supposed to be ironic, but his voice is hoarse, and I respond as though it's deadly serious.

I whimper. It's undeniably a pathetic, needy little sound.

Yes. I need that. Very much.

I'm not too proud to admit that Ivan pursuing me and giving me gifts was why I gave in and agreed to be his girlfriend. I'm only human. I want some comfort in my life, and being able to help my sisters felt good. But Feliks offering—even as a joke—to give tender and personal care? Loving, like a daddy? Yeah. That's worth a thousand necklaces I could sell. That's something I could fall for.

I'm pinned in place by my own stupid desires as Feliks eyes me, then deliberately sets aside his laptop and, grabbing the sunscreen, paces over to me.

I'm super aware of how tall and big he is compared to me. How he could overpower me easily, and we're all alone on this island, and though it should scare me, it doesn't. It's... Hot. Really, really, hot.

He uncaps the sunscreen and squirts a generous amount into his palm, then sets it aside and rubs his hands together. The sound is lewd and unmistakably suggestive. That white cream contrasts to his black-tattooed fingers and the slickness mirrors what's between my legs.

I'm caught in this thirst trap, helpless to do anything but stare.

"Don't be shy," he rasps, and the tension between us notches up. "Unless you'd rather do it yourself?"

I shake my head, but my hands are trembling as I open the sarong and let it fall to the floor. Then I'm bared to him, only insubstantial triangles of fabric covering my most private places.

"Mm." He gives a deep sound of masculine appreciation at the reveal of my bikini-clad body. "Good girl."

Oh god that feels amazing. Good girl. I can't remember when I was last praised like that. Hayley says thanks when I do stuff around the house, and it's nice when an essay is returned with ticks and "Good" or "Great!"

But to have someone—an experienced, worldly, rich and powerful man like Feliks, in particular—say it to me in person, with his deep voice? That's chocolate ice cream on a hot day.

Taking my hand in his, he smooths his palm up my arm and over my shoulder. I press my lips together to keep from making inappropriate noises as this huge man puts sunscreen on me with bold sweeps of his hands. First one arm, then the other.

He's not brisk or efficient, but neither does he linger in obvious seductiveness. Picking up the sunscreen again, he cups my shoulder with his big palm, and I turn with the slight pressure. His movement is confident as he clears the hair from my back, then passes his hand over my shoulders and down my back.

I didn't know sunscreen could be sexy, but I bite my bottom lip to stop the sound of how much I like this getting out when he reaches my hips. His hands are so big it barely takes any time for him to cover my back and certainly not as long as I'd like.

His touch is turning me to molten jelly, despite the air conditioning in this house.

When he wordlessly clasps my shoulder and turns me to face him again, I'm struck again by how enormous he is. I have to crane my neck to look up at him. Those dark-blue eyes are intense as he holds my gaze and slides down to kneel. We're almost face-to-face, me looking very slightly down. Which, of course, should make me feel dominant that he's knelt, but actually it only emphasises that he could crush me with one tattooed hand.

He pours more suncream into his hands and dips his gaze to my legs starting at my left ankle, and cupping my whole calf. I'm vibrating with how erotic this is.

I tingle all over as his hands get above my knee, then to mid-thigh. It's only when he reaches higher that I wonder if he'll take what I'm so obviously offering.

I hold my breath.

"Spread your legs for me, lisichka." His voice is gravelly as he nudges my inner thigh with the back of his hand.

Obediently, I shift my feet apart, but looking down, he moves slightly, and my eyes go wide as I see that his shorts are tented. That thick, hot length I had under my fingers earlier has returned, and it steals my breath.

But despite that, he rubs the suncream into the delicate skin of the top of my leg, apparently focused on his task, and not noticing the demand of his own body or the way I'm writhing with horny thoughts.

The bikini bottoms are at an angle over my bottom, and as his fingertips run along the seam between the fabric and my skin, I'm practically panting.

I want him to dip under the stretchy line and brush against my throbbing, heated, swollen clit. I can't press my legs together to get a bit of friction, and he's literally right in front of me so there's no way to writhe or reach between my legs and give myself relief.

But I'm getting so turned on.

My heart is beating fast as he starts again with my other leg, one palm easily enveloping the top of my foot. Then he slides his hands up my other leg, pausing to put more suncream into his palms, then at my inner thigh, I swear he slows.

He's holding my gaze, and I'm totally trapped by him. No handcuffs required for this captive. Apparently, sunscreen is all that's needed.

His hands encircle my thigh, giving it a subtle squeeze that I don't think I'd notice if I wasn't attuned to his every movement. It's as though there's a connection between us, an unseen thread of communication without words, where the slightest touch is a meeting of souls.

I try to tell myself that's absurd, and not true, but when he calmly removes his hands and picks the bottle of sunscreen back up, I'm bereft. I need him.

He grasps my waist almost like he's steadying me, and brings one hand around to my tummy, smearing white cream as he does. Then his palm rests there, his thumb swiping over my belly button.

His gaze is fixed on my lower stomach, but whereas with anyone else I'd think they were judging that it isn't flat and it's kind of pudgy, with Feliks there's something wistful in his dark expression that makes me wonder how it would feel to have his baby growing in my belly, and all his protective, possessive focus on me.

I squirm a little with the idea, the bright spark impossible to keep inside.

His face stays carefully neutral as he runs his hands up my ribcage. I can see what's going to happen before it does, and I hold my breath, keeping still so perhaps he won't notice when... Oh, yes. The side of his finger brushes the underside of the curve of my breast.

My heart is a tiny bird fluttering its wings.

Which is unfortunate, because Feliks moves his attention to the top of my chest.

And. Oof. Uh. This. Bikini. I thought it had a decent amount of coverage, but the triangles are miniature. Really, really, small. Compared to his hands, which cover my entire breast easily.

He smooths his fingers up and over my neck, stopping on my racing pulse. He's got a delicate touch for a man so big.

And when he unfolds himself and pushes up to his full height and dabs sunscreen on my face, I'm so conflicted.

I know he's seen how I'm responding to him, how I want him, but he's being utterly controlled. Far more appropriate than you could expect from a mafia boss, when I'm his captive.

I keep forgetting that.

"Close your eyes," he rumbles.

My heart lurches.

"What are you going to do?" I blurt out.

He takes a step closer, so I can feel the heat of his much larger body. Taking my chin in his forefinger and thumb, he holds me immobile.

"Whatever I want, Payton."

A shudder of desire racks me from head to toe.

"It's only you and me here, and you being a little brat won't change that you aren't just in my power. You're in my kingdom. You can't run, or hide, or escape. You're my prisoner, and I can do anything I like to you."

Please do.

"You belong to me, now, lisichka."

Yes.

"You will do what I tell you, sooner or later. You have no choice."

Why is that so hot?

"So. Close." His voice goes dark and smoky. "Your. Eyes."

9

PAYTON

Those fluttery-soft butterflies return to my belly as I let my eyelids fall.

"That's my good girl," he croons.

There's a wet noise, and he exhales and releases my chin.

Because of the bright sunlight coming through the windows, it's not black behind my eyelids. There are blotches of pink and orange. But there isn't what I want to see, which is Feliks.

The sound of the air conditioning unit and the call of birds outside is louder, and my skin prickles with apprehension.

I sway, and catch another scent, beneath the suncream's floral notes with a metallic tang, there's a musky note that's deeper, and almost woody.

Feliks.

He hasn't touched me since I closed my eyes, but when I bite my lip, he chuckles softly.

My nipples have pebbled. I know it. Not knowing where he's looking, or if he's even watching me, makes this unbearable. The moment stretches out, and I wonder if he somehow moved away and left me like this, craving him, so horny, and needing... Something. Him. I haven't done enough with other men—boys—to be sure what I'm on the edge of.

I gasp as his hand clasps my jaw, and then I feel his fingers on my other cheek, over my eyebrow, down the side of my face and over my brow.

It takes a second for the obvious to hit me.

Sunscreen.

Of course. He's putting it on my face, and ensuring it doesn't go in my eyes.

"That's it," he murmurs as I tilt my chin up into his touch.

He wipes the cream over my cheeks, and down the bridge of my nose. This is the most intimate thing that has ever been done to me. His finger on my upper lip, and under my eye is a depth of trust I didn't even realise that I hadn't given anyone.

With my eyes shut, I'm mesmerised by the path of his touch, his breath that I imagine I can feel on my hair, and the extreme vulnerability of not being able to see what he's doing, or what to expect next.

His hands lift, and I wait, longing for what he promised. Whatever he wants to do to me.

I'm his doll. His to dress, protect, care for. Direct.

"Perfect." He takes a deep breath and lets it out. "You can open your eyes now."

He's stepped away, and my whole being slumps with disappointment. I disguise it with a smile. "Thank you. Can I go swim?"

"Should I call you little fish, instead?" he asks indulgently as he nods, but I'm already scurrying out of the house and onto the decking.

"What do you mean, instead?" The moment my feet touch the sand though, I squeal.

Feliks laughs, and doesn't answer my question.

It's burning hot, scorching the soles of my feet, and I hop in disbelief. It's insanely hot!

"Such a soft creature," Feliks says, calmly walking over the roasting sand.

The desire to watch his retreating back battles with the pain from my feet, and self-preservation wins out over thirst. I make a dash for the water, sprinting as fast as I can, my feet on fire, and when I reach the sea, it's heaven.

The water laps at my feet and I groan with relief. But it's not freezing, like the outdoor pools are at home in London. I take another step. It's Goldilocks water, the temperature of bathwater when you've read two chapters and yawn sleepily.

Feliks splashes into the sea next to me.

"How are your feet not char-grilled?" I ask.

He shrugs. "Practice. You swimming?"

He's already up to his waist, ahead of me, and my god, his tattooed, muscled back is as stunning as the view. All stark black lines and golden skin. He's at home here, like he said.

An elegant dive and he emerges in motion, shaking the water from his hair and cutting through with easy strokes. I watch him, the sun on my skin, the water lapping at my ankles, the soft sand beneath my feet, and the salty scent of the ocean in my nose.

There's a line further out where the turquoise near the beach deepens to dark-blue the colour of Feliks' eyes. And I recognise why he seems like he was made out of this place.

The golden sand his skin and the deep sea his eyes. The black of his hair and his tattoos is all his own though.

He stops and turns, treading water and smooths the hair out of his eyes.

"Come on. You wanted to swim," he teases.

I did, but apparently, I want to look at him, and be touched by him even more.

"You're distracting," I mutter under my breath, but I follow him in, bracing myself for the inevitable cold... But unlike home, it's not. It's perfect.

The water envelops me, and in seconds I'm in and swimming, ducking my head under water and just the right amount of cool washes over me.

I love swimming anywhere for the joy of my body being held, weightless. There aren't jarring knocks to my knees or my ankles when I swim as there are when I run. My boobs aren't an inconvenience, in fact, nothing about my body is wrong in the water. I swear Taylor got all the graceful Love genes, and I got all the awkward ones.

I pause and look down through the perfectly clear water. I can even see the sand at the bottom.

"There's no coral here?"

"On the other side of the island," Feliks says. "If you can learn to equalise your ears, I'll take you diving."

"Really?" I say, surprised.

"Of course."

"But why?" We're both treading water, perhaps six feet apart now.

"You're my prisoner to protect you, as I said. Not as punishment or torture."

I think of what he told me about Ivan, and it's the first chill I've had since we landed. Feliks is floating nearby, and

I spin in the water so I'm on my back and take a few lazy strokes, propelling myself from the beach.

It's picture-perfect as I look up at the afternoon sky and back at the beach house, palm trees, and curve of the sand around the corner.

We're on the edge of the darker-blue water now, and I begin to paddle away from Feliks. All I can see of him is his head, his shoulders and body all hidden by the water.

"Not too far out, lisichka," Feliks says.

"Why? Worried I'll escape?" I turn and look over my shoulder. "Is that another island in the distance?" It's difficult to make out from here, but there's a line of cloud on the horizon that could be land.

"I wouldn't want you to get into trouble," he answers gravely.

"Hum." I make a sing-sonny teasing noise. "I think you just don't want me to escape."

I can swim well, but that far? I'm not sure. Maybe enough to get around the island, and find a way to get a message to Hayley. She'll be freaking out by now. If we can dive on the other side of the island, maybe there's diving equipment and other stuff there. A boat, for instance.

Casually, I swim away.

"Lisichka," he says warningly.

"What does that mean?" I ask again, continuing to put distance between us, but his eyes are gleaming, and he's following.

"Little fox." I paddle a bit faster, turning to aim around the island rather than straight out to sea. Might I be quicker than Feliks? It's unlikely, but right now I have the element of surprise. He doesn't know what I'm going to do.

"Why a little fox?" I'm keeping talking to him to lull

him into a false sense of security, not because I want the answer to why he's given me a cute pet name.

"Because you're clever, and quick, and beautiful," he replies.

I glow with the compliment.

"But, little fox, although you can swim very well, you should be aware..." There's something in his expression. Something feral and dangerous and arrogantly in control.

I bolt, launching my body into an efficient front crawl. My head goes down and I pound my arms through the water, kicking desperately.

He swears, and there's a splashing sound.

I don't look back, my heart racing.

I focus on breathing, my face snapping from one side to the other, dragging in air. The sun is hot, and yeah, there's not much of a chance, but really? I have to take this opportunity, scant as it is.

For a moment I think I might escape. It's a stupid, fleeting thought, born of blood that's pounding and legs and arms already screaming at me.

Then something catches at my ankle. Hard.

I know it's Feliks before my body does, and I flail as I come to a sudden stop and I'm sinking, my head going under, and my foot staying up, my bottom awkwardly sagging in the middle.

Then I'm hauled against a warm chest, and Feliks' hands are under my armpits, holding me.

I cough and splutter, my hair over my eyes and despite knowing I'm caught, I push against his shoulders. Then my legs have tangled with his and my brain is putty.

"I'm a shark. And I will catch you every time you try to escape, my naughty little fox."

Pulling in breath, I glare at him.

I knew he'd catch me. I think I wanted him to.

Holding me to him with one arm, he tucks the wet tendrils of my hair behind my ear.

"Moya lisichka. You're such trouble." There's exasperation in his tone, but he grips me tighter, and without thinking, I wrap my legs around his waist. He's effortlessly keeping both of us afloat in the deep, blue sea.

That's the other thing about the water. It's a leveller. Where on the ground, he towers over me, here he's just a head. My imagination fills in all the details I saw earlier, but we're face-to-face.

I'm still breathing hard as I look into Feliks' eyes, and all the crackling tension between us pulls in, like a thunderstorm cloud rolling over the horizon, low and unavoidable. My inner thighs, the ones he so carefully covered with sunscreen, are clamped onto him. Where I thought I was trying to lever myself away with my hands on his shoulders, I'm gripping him, exploring the top of his back with my fingertips. The sun through the water droplets on my eyelashes and on his face cover everything with sparkles and rainbows.

Suddenly, it's not the chase and capture that has my heart racing, it's him.

Feliks. My ex-boyfriend's dad.

It took months of Ivan badgering me, giving me gifts, and generally not taking no for an answer before I let him kiss me. And even then, it was a sad, tepid kiss. Closed lips. Passionless. I didn't want it, and I don't think, from what Feliks said, that Ivan did either.

But less than a day with his dad, and I'm almost ready to beg for a kiss.

"You've my captive, and that means you can't leave. But anything else, Payton, that's up to you. So if you don't want me to kiss you, you need to move away. Because being so close to you? I can't trust myself. You're too beautiful. Too tempting. Too sweet and perfect for a man like me. And right now, you're still my son's girlfriend."

"Ex-girlfriend." It's a little puff of air, barely even words.

"Until I kill him," he says harshly. "Think carefully about your answer. Consider what you're going to do next, but don't take too long because I'll have my lips on yours."

I can't, because I crave whatever this is. I'm hot and needy between my legs and my lips are tingling with desire.

"I'll give you a countdown. Three." He leans closer, his warm breath on my lips. "Two." Angling his head, he raises his hand and slides his fingertips over my jaw. "One."

Then his lips reach mine.

10

FELIKS

This is what I've needed since I first saw Payton. In my arms, yielding, sweet, and her mouth on mine. Her lips taste salty from the sea, but they're soft, and as soon as I withdraw the smallest amount from the kiss, she makes a needy, breathy sound like, "Uhh".

It shoots arousal right into my already painfully erect cock.

I tighten my hold on her as I tread water to keep us afloat, and close the gap again, taking her lips with mine.

This time it's a glide, a lure. I crave deeper, darker, more possessive intimacy with Payton, but this is my invitation and promise to her.

I will make this as good as you deserve, if you just trust me. Her perfect little tits press to my chest, and I long to rip off her bikini and see her nipples. Feel how they pucker from my attention, and hear her cry out with pleasure.

The soft changes to her breathing are gratifying though. I keep teasing her lips with mine, rather than plundering her as I'd like to. My tongue in her mouth, my cock in her tight pussy.

"Feliks," she moans, and writhes against me.

"Moya lisichka."

I suck gently on her plush bottom lip and the whimpers, distract me so much I stop swimming for a moment, and she giggles as both our chins are submerged before I kick and get us higher in the water.

"I need to kiss you somewhere that if I get carried away, no one will drown," I mutter against her lips, but I don't stop. I'm drifting us towards the beach, and dabbing my tongue over her lips. And when she opens, I take. Sliding my tongue into her mouth is far filthier and better with Payton than anything I can remember.

Acceptance of this girl I shouldn't touch, shouldn't have, is heady.

She's mine. The thought is raw and primal, as intense as the instinct to chase her down when she tried to swim away.

Mine. Mine to protect, mine to care for, mine to pleasure until she's wrung out and exhausted.

Her tongue meets mine, and the salty, wet slide makes my mouth water. I need more.

One of my hands shifts up, almost without my say-so, and cups the back of her head, bringing her closer to me. Angling our heads so I can kiss her deeper, I let myself just feel this moment of her in my arms, in the sea where I caught her, with no questions because our tongues are dancing together. The water is soft and warm, the top few inches heated compared to the cooler currents that swirl around my legs.

Later is the time for doubt on her side, and guilt on mine.

With every second that passes I'm more certain that leaving Payton is impossible, and not keeping close will break me.

I crush her to me, and this kiss has gone feral. My cock is aching for the relief of being in her, an iron bar between us. Undeniable. And there's an unexpected hunger too.

I'd like to breed this girl.

Not a thought I've ever had before. I kick steadily to keep us both afloat, but that's not what steals all the breath from my lungs. No, it's the idea of sending jets of seed up into her fertile womb. It's a fiery craving that burns at my skin like the tropical sun drying the seawater on my face and baking on the salt. Bind her to me. Make a family, deliberately. A wife and children I'd protect and nurture.

Payton seems innocent, but the eager way she kisses me now that she's in my arms tells me how we'd be together. Explosive.

I ease my hand down until it's holding her bottom, and she's grinding against the length of my erection in time to the sway of the water. And perhaps it's the curve of her peachy little arse that snaps my self-control. Because a kiss isn't enough.

I need to feel her come, and we're too far out to do that.

Gripping her hair in my fist, I separate our mouths and look into her eyes. Pale-blue as the horizon, and just as clear.

My cock throbs with demand.

"Did you like it when I swam after you?" I ask simply.

Her mouth falls open, a perfect little pink "O". Her lips are wet and pink, and a bit swollen from the intensity of our kiss.

"Did I...?" She blinks.

I tug her hair, pulling her head back to reveal her sensitive neck.

She lets out a little cry, and her hips writhe against me.

"When we're on dry land, I'm going to make you scream. But I'm reasonable." I'm not. "I'll give you a chance to get away, what, to the other side of the island?" I have a suspicion what we'll find if we go there, and it's not just the diving spot. Her pupils are blown despite the sun.

Payton gets a look that I'm beginning to recognise. She's planning something. "I need a head start."

"Of course." I release her, and she pushes away.

"When I'm halfway to the beach, you can come after me."

I grin. I enjoy a challenge, and moya lisichka clearly thinks she's fast.

"Go on then." I judge the distance. I'll get her. "Ten, nine." Her eyes go wide, and then she hurls herself through the water. And however quick I thought she was before, I'm impressed now. She doesn't hold anything back, swimming with a smooth, efficient stroke that's almost as fast as mine.

I smile as I keep counting down, speaking louder so she can hear me.

This girl. She's stronger than she looks, and she's motivated.

So am I.

My muscles vibrate with the need to get after her. To seize her. To have her in my arms again after a chase.

She's going to make me work for this.

I wonder if I'll manage to catch her in the water? I assumed I would, but as I count, "Four, three, two," I'm not sure, and sprinting along the sand becomes a very real prospect. "One. I'm coming for you, lisichka."

I take my first powerful stroke, kicking like hell, and sending me forwards. Then I'm head down. Focused on swimming as fast as possible, every muscle working in rhythm, with a single aim.

Get her. Pin her. Make her mine.

There's tranquillity in the pursuit. My mind is clear of

anything but the water around me and the desire to capture my girl.

The salt. The sun. My world in the shape of a forbidden woman half my age. But this is utter clarity when presented with a choice of whether to allow her to put herself in danger, or force her into my arms? There's no question.

My cock is still as stiff as a bat, which probably accounts more for why I'm not faster. I'm swimming with a fucking anchor dragging, and no oxygen going to my limbs that really need it.

But there's no way my cock is getting the message. It has main character syndrome, and thinks chasing Payton is entirely for horny reasons.

There's just my heart pounding in my chest as I slice through the sea, the colour turning pale-turquoise as I reach the area closer to the beach.

Salty water clarifies everything. Tears. Blood. The ocean. And right now, it has revealed to me that no matter what the price is, Payton belongs to me.

My eyes sting as I look up to check where she is, and fuck. Moya lisichka is a wily little thing.

She's scrambling to her feet ahead of me. I'll be faster than her on solid ground, with my longer, stronger legs. But what if she gets to the house in time to make mischief? Lock me out perhaps?

Pizdets, I cannot let that happen.

I push harder. My chest heaves. My arms are screaming as I hear her splashing.

Got to get her. Then the water is shallow, and I'm on my feet and pounding after her, spray flying everywhere.

I've gained. A lot. But she's probably six paces ahead.

Her dripping wet, bikini-clad body is a sight I'll have burned into my retinas for the rest of my life.

I home in on her, my taller frame eating up the ground far quicker.

The soft sand makes it hard going for us both, but more so for her, with her shorter frame meaning more steps.

I've never run like this. I've never chased, either, and it's sheer willpower that forces my lactic-acid-filled legs faster, closing the gap between us.

Then she's at the patio door, pulling it open, my feet slapping on the wooden deck, and as she slips inside, I barge in with her. Wrapping one arm around her waist, I propel us across the room, falling onto the sofa, me under her to break her fall before I roll over and pin her squirming body with my hips.

Pinning her, I look down into her blue eyes.

Mine.

11

FELIKS

I'm still hard. My cock presses into the space between her thighs, and jerks in response to her.

We're both wet and sandy. I'm dripping seawater onto her. She's slippery beneath me. But my shock at the intensity of the feelings between us is mirrored on her face.

"What were you going for?" My hips hold her down, but she's not scratching at my eyes, or trying to really get away.

Her gaze flicks to my suit jacket on the kitchen island. Where both our phones are tucked into my pockets.

"Ah, your phone." I lift myself from her and in two steps I have her phone in my hand. It's switched off, as my men are well trained. No leaving live devices around.

"You like games, don't you?" I toss and catch it.

Sitting up on the sofa, Payton regards me with a mixture of hope and despair. In that little bikini, sopping wet, she looks good enough to eat.

"I have to contact my sister," she pleads.

I nearly give in. Grabbing my own phone, I click it open

to my messages with my core team. There are a series of updates on their search for Ivan.

They still haven't found him.

I look at Payton's phone, and the girl herself, her eyes pleading. She can't use her phone. Even opening it would trigger off any spyware Ivan has, and since he's still at large, he could get here. And calling her sister from mine is asking for trouble. A second sister going missing? Hayley will be raising every alarm, and that means the meddling London "Maths" Club, who try to get involved with every cat stuck up a tree in London, and will make it their mission to "rescue" her. Tracing us to this island will be easy.

She's everything to me.

I can't risk it. Her.

"Here's my deal. If you don't beg, you can have the phone." I place it on the top of a high shelf that her cute little self won't be able to reach. "I enjoy a challenge."

And Payton is a worthy opponent, for all her youth. She was a faster swimmer than I expected, and I'm excited to bend her to my will. To show her that letting me lead is better for her, and that I'll take care of her better than she can.

"You're going to torture me?" She swallows nervously.

I cross my arms, restrain my grin, and stare down at her.

"Your choice is that the phone goes in the sea, or you accept my deal, and try not to beg." I take my tie from where I discarded it.

"Okay." She tilts her chin up bravely, and that only makes her even more appealing to me. She's sitting primly, with her knees together and her hands folded in her lap. It's a transparent effort to cover her amazing tits, and seem small and unthreatening. I guess she really thinks I'm going to hurt her.

"Put your hands above your head," I tell her.

She licks her lips, and for a second, I think she'll protest. But she doesn't, and the air goes thick and hot as I watch her raise her arms.

"Good girl." Her eyelids flutter. She likes that, huh? My girl enjoys being appreciated, and I can deliver all of the praise she needs.

I approach, and it's a thrill when her gaze drops from my face to the bulge in my shorts, and her cheeks pinken.

With deliberate, slow movements so I don't scare her, but I do make it clear who's in charge now, I drop one knee on either side of her thighs and lean over her. Wrapping my tie around her wrists, I bind them tightly enough she'll feel it, and can't escape, but it's a long way from hurting.

I'd die before I'd harm her.

I nudge her hands down until they're resting on the back of the sofa behind her head, then rise again to stand in front of her, looking down.

I'm tall and imposing. But I think she likes that, because her gaze bounces around my body, taking in my many tattoos.

"Spread your legs for me."

"What?" she says, breathily.

"Open them wide, so I can see the edges of your pretty little cunt."

She whimpers at the crudeness of my words, but obediently parts her thighs.

The bikini bottoms cover what I really want, and this angle isn't right, but I'll take it.

I nod with approval.

"Now what?" she asks with an edge of defiance and a quiver of fear.

"I'm going to make you beg and scream."

"Or I might nap," she replies, and it takes visible effort.

I chuckle and grab a cushion from the sofa, tossing it onto the floor at our feet. When I lower myself down, her brow furrows with confusion.

"My knees will be murder otherwise," I confess, and she blinks. "I intend on being down here a *long time*, and if you're going to be a stubborn brat, it might be even longer."

I pluck at one bow of her bikini bottoms, and she gasps as it falls apart.

I smirk. Perfect. Easy access.

Tugging at the other one, it gives up too, and with a flick of the fabric, she's revealed to me. I grab her thighs with both hands and tug. That modest pose with her little arse tucked in under her won't do. I need her sprawled, and her cunt where I can get my lips on it.

She squeaks in surprise, and I just admire the creamy skin of her legs from this new perspective. A pink flower, but wet and succulent. She's even served on a damn plate of her bikini. She couldn't be any better if she tried.

My mouth waters. She's going to be delicious.

I'd like to see her tits as well, and fuck it. I shouldn't, but there's nothing okay about what I'm doing. She's a lovely twenty-one-year-old girl who got caught up in trouble she didn't understand. I'm a Bratva boss, with hundreds of men at my command and a kill tally snaking around my bicep.

I tug up the triangles of fabric and reveal her berry-pink nipples. This can't work, but I can take this one thing. Her orgasm.

I lean down and inhale the sweetness of her pussy juices, the evidence I need that she wants this too, and salt water.

"Feliks!" she squawks.

My head is up in a split second. I can't disguise my concern. "Payton?"

She gulps and I run a comforting hand over her splayed knee.

"I..." She tails off and looks away.

Fuck. No.

"What did he do to you?" My voice is gentle, but there's steel behind it. As though I need more reasons to kill Ivan, but I have to know.

"Nothing," she says in a pained tone. "No one's ever done anything."

My heart swells at the same time the relief eases my joints loose again.

"I don't know what to do," she whispers. "And what if I lose because of being a virgin and getting it wrong?"

My sweet girl is still worried about her sister.

"Lisichka, experience wouldn't help you. And it will be my honour to be the first to eat your tasty little cunt until you come."

"Oh!" Her eyes go wide. "That's what you meant?"

"That's the game," I confirm. "I tease you until you beg me. You try to hold out." I run my palm up her leg, then back down, and she shivers. "Agree?"

Her silence is enough for me. I bring my mouth down and take a greedy lick all the way up her folds and groan because she's even softer and sweeter than I imagined, with the salt of the sea too.

Her lips jerk, and she lets out a surprised squeak.

I chuckle, and flick my tongue on her clit. "I know, and it's going to get better, trust me."

Caressing her thighs, I lap her juices, working out and back in again, but only glancingly sweeping her clit. I urge her legs further apart to make room for me to see all of her, really spread out. My new favourite meal is this girl. She makes soft noises of pleasure and shifts impatiently as I take my time to explore every inch of her pussy and thighs with my tongue and lips.

I build her ecstasy carefully, finding the exact place and speed she prefers. Feeling her respond to me as I drive her higher and higher has my cock aching for relief.

But she's my priority, and the way she moans and writhes is so good. An unexpected connection when I'd assumed I would never care about another person as much as I do myself. To discover that half my soul is in an innocent girl is as shocking and the feeling that so long as she comes, it doesn't matter if I don't.

If she trusts me, and will beg for me, that's everything.

I take my time, and get her to the edge of pleasure, when she's bucking into me, chasing the next firm lick.

And then I stop.

She keens, vibrating with need, and I know I've got her to the brink.

"I'll let you come. One more touch, and you'll be there. I can give it to you." I want to. Maybe I crave it even more than she does.

"You bastard!" she sobs out.

"It's to keep you safe," I tell her honestly.

"I can't, I have to..." She writhes in her restraints. "I..." There are more babbling words. Incoherent.

"Say the word, Payton."

She hesitates, not ready. Still holding out.

I sit back on my heels and my knees crack. Fuck, as though I needed that reminder I'm forty-four. "I think I'm thirsty."

"What?" she pants. "You *what*? You're going to leave me like this?"

"Only for a moment." I pause meaningfully. "When you've calmed down a bit, and I've had a glass of water, I'll resume."

She makes a high-pitched noise of frustration and desire.

"Unless you have something you want to say to me?"

"No, no... I..." She shakes her head and tugs against the tie holding her hands, but she doesn't attempt to touch herself, close her legs, or escape.

She's such a pretty sight, her cunt all on display for me. I rise to my full height.

"Are you going to be a good girl while I get us some refreshment?"

She sobs and rolls her hips, but nods her head.

"This house has solar panels on the roof and a battery system," I explain as I fetch a pint glass and fill it with ice and cold water from the fridge. "We have all we need to do this for as long as required."

I take a long glug and sigh contentedly as I look back at Payton.

She's biting her bottom lip, eyes screwed closed as though in pain.

"Just ask me." I refill the glass and return to her.

She opens her eyes and the mixture of defiance and desire I see there only serves to harden my cock to steel.

"I can't." But it's a tired refusal.

"Do you want water?" I bet she's as thirsty as I am after being in the sea. And all that whimpering.

"If I say yes, is that begging, and I lose?" she asks suspiciously.

I shake my head. "You're missing the point of this entirely, Payton."

"What is it then? Because I thought it was to torture me until I beg you to stop."

"It's to force you to let me care for you and protect you the way I know you need, and not allow you to get into trouble," I reply, low and simply with the truth of the statement.

She blinks and tilts her face down, hiding her reaction.

Interesting.

I drop a knee and then straddle her again. She gives a squeak of protest, but I just tip her chin up with one finger, and murmur, "Open."

She obeys.

I take a sip of water and drop my head until my lips touch hers. Slowly, I let a stream flow into her mouth.

Lowering her chin so she can swallow, I bend so I look her straight in those pretty blue eyes.

"Trust me to provide for you. Ask me. Beg me. And I will. I want to, in every way."

Her pulse is fluttering at her throat, and she nods.

"Good girl." I put the glass to her lips and help her drink until she's had enough.

"Thank you," she murmurs, a little shyly.

"It's my pleasure, lisichka." I move off the sofa and kneel again at my place at her feet. "Now, back to this delicious pussy."

She shudders and cries out as I lick her again, not starting slowly this time.

"I still want you to trust me and beg me to let you come," I explain patiently, then dive back, face-first into the heaven between her legs.

So even as my knees hurt, my shoulders ache, and my tongue cramps, I don't stop. I just add in my fingers, a tiny bit at a time, one fingertip, then up to a knuckle, building her up to two ramming into her, stroking her inside and out.

I push her to the edge over and over, pausing when she's about to come, and sitting back. My hands are covered with her cream. It's all over my cheeks.

"You look so sexy like this." I stroke around her clit, deliberately avoiding the throbbing nub.

I don't know how long we've been going now, but between her arousal and my licking her, the bikini bottoms under her are soaked.

She's moaning incoherently, but she's not begging.

It almost hurts me not to make her come. I'm so hard my erection could break rocks.

It's on the tip of my tongue to say that she can call her sister as soon as my men have found Ivan.

That would be the kind thing to do, a compromise.

But I started with this, and although I'm being an unreasonable arsehole, I need her to submit to me.

I stroke her hair with one hand as she breaks down, almost crying.

"Poor desperate lisichka." I trail my hand up her inner thigh. "Your cunt is so pretty. Genuinely the sweetest I've ever tasted, and my god, the way you're so responsive. You're a miracle."

I ruthlessly push two fingers into her impossibly tight passage, so hot and slick I know I won't last long when my cock is finally lodged inside there. Rubbing that patch at the top of her opening makes her crazy, drawing out little whimper from her as I thrust in again and again, curling to get her to that moment where she could topple.

Then I feel it. She's wound so tight, she's gripping my knuckles, shaking all over. So close to orgasm it's heavy in the air.

I lift away my head, leaving my fingers inside her.

"Ask," I command her as she whines in frustration at the

removal of my mouth. Stroking her knee soothingly, I look into her pale-blue eyes.

They beg me, plead. But she presses her lips together as though without that effort, the words might escape and jump into the air.

She's getting a little bit puffy on her clit and the pink folds that I've enjoyed paying devout attention to have nearly taken all the stimulation they can.

A blade of doubt cuts at me.

"You're so beautiful, and you've been so strong."

I press kisses to her belly, and while I wish it was a promise to put a baby in there, this girl might be stubborn enough to break both of us.

"Please," I whisper. "Let me give you this."

I'm begging. I'm the one fucking begging.

She doesn't respond, and my heart sinks.

Fuck. Okay.

I know when I'm beaten. I was so sure, and I clench my jaw at the risk I've let her take. I'll give her my phone, and accept the consequences.

The thought that in the inevitable fight she might be taken away from me cracks me apart. I'm not sure I can deal with this honourably.

I push to my feet, but as soon as I've turned, heading for the shelf where her phone is stashed, I hear a little voice.

"Feliks." There's a new need there, desperate, and reluctant.

"Lisichka." I don't move. I don't dare hope.

"Please."

Relief surges in me.

"Please, what?" I keep my tone measured and calm.

"Please..." Her breath hitches. "Please make me come."

12

FELIKS

I don't need asking twice, or to draw out my victory by making her beg more.

Half a second and I'm between her legs again, holding her hips down with one arm and shoving my fingers into her with the other, getting my mouth onto that sweet flesh as quickly as I can.

She screams as she comes, just as I said she would. Long and loud. And as she quakes in the aftermath, I smile. So fucking happy that I get to feel her orgasm. Even better that I did it. I made her come all over my face.

When she's exhausted and over sensitised, destroyed by being edged over and over then exploding into pleasure, I give in. Shoving down my shorts, I have my rock-solid erection in my hand before I've considered. I shouldn't. But I have the most primal need to mark her.

"Eating your tight little cunt has been the ultimate turn on," I confess hoarsely, clambering to stand over her. "I can't wait any longer."

My fingers are slick from her pussy juices, and I groan as the pleasure raps between the base of my spine and the sensitive helmet of my cock. I'm primed, ready to come already, balls pulled up.

"So good." I drag my gaze over her body. "Your tits..." I'm almost as incoherent with need as she was at the end. "Perfect. My good girl for coming like that. So strong to hold out."

She's young and innocent, watching me with her eyes as wide as dinner plates. Her eyes flits between my face and my erection, seemingly unable to choose.

I work my cock hard and fast, my fingers tight. It's sharp and so sweet, this pleasure. It has the knife edge of how fucking filthy and perverted I am.

Laid back on the sofa as she is, her cheeks flushed, her tits exposed, her hair drying in cute frizz on her shoulders and her legs still spread wide, she's the ultimate temptation.

Using brutal, desperate pumps of my hand, it's a race against time. If I don't come quickly, I'll shove my cock in that delicate, puffy pink cunt of hers, or order her to open her mouth again and spurt down her throat.

"You're so big," she breathes. "Even bigger than I thought. Feliks..."

My name on her lips is the trigger I need.

My orgasm erupts, the base starting the wave of ecstasy that rolls up my length and then I'm pumping white fluid over her.

I don't hold back. I spray her with it, exploding in ropes over her pussy. Her stomach. Those pert little tits I'd like to fuck. By the fourth pulse I shift forward and it sprays over her shocked face.

I roar as I come all over her, in a blatantly territorial claiming.

She isn't my son's. She's not leaving me. She belongs to me, and I want everyone to know it. She's *mine* to protect.

It racks through me, releasing all the pent-up need from hours of wanting her. I come a copious amount, milking every drop onto her skin. Somewhere in the waves of pleasure, there's a truth that I can't admit. This is unlike anything I've ever felt.

Payton's mouth is an "O" as she watches me, pink cheeked.

This time I sink down next to her on the sofa.

Bracing my forearm beside her head, I lean over her, and trail my hand down her neck to where her bikini top is rucked up. There's a splash of white liquid there, and I smear it.

"I imagined this when I put suncream on you," I grit out.

She whimpers softly. My lizard brain keeps my fingers moving. Massaging it in like I did earlier.

I continue down, my mind clear in the same way as it was when I chased her as I work my semen into her skin. Thoroughly.

I want it so deep into her it won't wash off. So she feels me in her as I do her. I don't know how, but there was a Payton-shaped space in my heart, and she slotted right into it.

"You're so beautiful," I mutter. I'm compulsively rubbing it into her stomach now, moving across her skin until she's shiny with it everywhere.

Except, there's some sprayed between her legs, and as I touch her there, her breathing goes ragged again.

I pause. It's one thing to put my come over her belly and imagine that part of her growing with my child. It's another to push that seed over the pretty folds of her pussy.

"Only just orgasmed, but you're a needy little thing, aren't you?" I say under my breath. "Do you want more?"

"Feliks, please. Touch me."

I'm lightheaded with her words as I slide my fingers over her clit and she moans.

"Shall I finger you with this? Can you feel the slippery, dirty, naughtiness of it?" I rub her little bud and smile as she bucks her hips.

"Yes. Please."

"Good girl for asking." I intensify the pressure around her clit, feeling for exactly the right amount. "I like it when you use your words."

"Oh!" She throws her head back.

I murmur my approval, and switch to Russian as I pour out the excessive thoughts I've had since we met. That I want her to have my children. Be my wife. That I'd lay down my life for her if needed, but I fear I'd do much harder things too.

I describe how she makes me want to be a better man, but at the same time, by taking what I most desire—her—I'm being my worst self.

She's irresistible.

There's a splash of semen on her face, and as she gets close to coming, I smooth it over her cheek and paint it over her lips.

Then her tongue wets her bottom lip, and I instinctively nudge my finger into her mouth.

And that's when she cries out, a climax that sparks from me invading her.

I ease off for her, nudging at the side of her clit to draw out her orgasm more.

My heartbeat thuds heavily, and I'm nervous for a second as I reach above her head and undo the binding, releasing her wrists. I half expect her to move away, but she lets her arms fall, and when I pull her with me as I lie back, she comes without hesitation snuggling onto my chest when I urge her. She's sticky with my seed, and her cream, and I wouldn't have her any other way. I wrap my arms around her.

"We've wrecked your sofa," she says after a moment.

"Improved." I drop a kiss on the top of her head, and a tightness in my heart eases. It's been there for so long I didn't even realise it could dissolve. I thought that painful knot was a twisted part of who I am. What I've done.

But no. All the violence and rage are gone. All that's left is a need to protect this girl.

"With sea water and sand and..." She huffs with embarrassment.

"I'll get you another one, and make a mess of that sofa too." My mouth quirks up into a contented

smile.

There's a pause as we both acknowledge that I'm talking about the future with a presumption that probably isn't justified given I kidnapped her mere hours ago.

All the reasons this is doomed scroll through my head.

She's my son's girlfriend. She's half my age. I abducted her. Her consent in this has been dubious at best. I've always been alone, I've never loved anyone, not even my own son. I don't know anything about caring for another person. I'm not a sadist like Ivan, but I'm far from being a good man.

She lives in Richmond, whose Kingpin is part of the London mafia syndicate, who aren't exactly friends of mine. In fact, they're my rivals and enemies, as well as the sort of idiots to get involved with a kidnapping that has nothing to do with them. Except that living in Richmond, Payton *is* their business. And her sister, too.

Fuck. A problem for tomorrow.

I breathe in the scent of her hair, then adjust us so I can push to my feet with her in my arms, bridal style, with one arm beneath her knees. She doesn't object when I take her to the shower, strip her naked, and wash every inch of her. Neither of us say anything when she's looking up into my face and I let my fingers trail down between her legs.

This time, I don't tease. And when her little hands find my throbbing cock—apparently my body thinks I'm a teenager again—it can't last long. I have to brace against the tiles because the feeling of her is too good.

Jet lag catches up with us both as we dry off from the shower, and we collapse into bed, her tucked into my chest, my arm over her waist. Too tired to talk about what the morning might bring.

13

PAYTON

I wake being tugged between utter contentment, and heavy guilt.

Feliks is holding me to him, his chest to my back, us both lying on our sides. He breathes slow and even, and though you could easily interpret the way his arm is snug on my waist as imprisoning, it just feels protective. And last night, my god. Thinking about yesterday makes me all squishy inside. Between my legs heats.

I've never experienced being really wanted. The way he edged me, but also covered me with sunscreen to protect me.

Being chased. I didn't know I'd love that either.

And this beach and house that feels more like home than anywhere I've ever lived, his honesty on the plane, and yeah mind-blowing orgasms don't hurt. Of course they don't.

But weighted against that is that my arrogant arsehole kidnapper won't let me call my sister, and Hayley will be going nuts with worry.

Dawn is just breaking out of the window, but because of the time difference, I'm awake. And perhaps being more used to making the trip, Feliks is still asleep.

I think of my phone on that top shelf in the lounge.

Could I? Dare I? I have to. After losing Taylor, Hayley will be distraught over me going missing.

I shift forward, and Feliks' grip on my waist tightens. That's not romantic, I try to tell myself. It's not sweet.

Smoothing my hand over his forearm, I lift it off, and he grumbles in his sleep.

"I'm just going to the loo," I whisper the lie as I creep out of his protective embrace and the light blanket.

He growls again, but when I tuck the covers over his shoulders, he accepts it, and his eyes remain closed, long lashes fanning his cheek.

I tiptoe across the room, waiting for him to wake and stop me, but he doesn't. Miraculously, somehow, when I turn the door handle and look back, he's motionless. The bedroom is dark because of the blinds that Feliks shut last night, and there's the hum of air conditioning, so I pray that he won't hear me or notice I'm gone.

I shut the door softly behind me, and pad silently to where Feliks stashed my phone.

I can't reach, of course, that was the point. But there are lower shelves, and I'm not that heavy. I consider a chair, but I'm hyper aware Feliks could wake at any second. Moving furniture from the other side of the room is riskier because it'll take longer, and the wood appears solid.

I go for it, putting one foot gingerly onto the bottom shelf and testing it. It holds. Of course it does. Everything in Feliks' life is made of premium materials.

I take the next step up more quickly, then another,

hanging onto the edge of the bookshelf. Ooo, is that a copy of…? No, I cannot get distracted.

I climb one more then snatch the phone and skip back down, heart thumping in my chest like our neighbour's music at the house in Richmond.

My finger is pressing the power button as I hear a door handle turn.

Shit shit shit.

No pockets in these night shorts, and what if he checks for the phone? I don't think. I just scale the bookshelves as quickly and nimbly as I can, slide it into place, and hop to the ground. As Feliks rounds the corner, I'm staring out at the ocean tinged with pale-yellow light from the sunrise.

"Lisichka," he says warningly. "What are you doing?"

"Looking at the beach," I say innocently, turning to him. And oof. He is somehow even hotter in the cool of the morning than he was last night. He's naked except for a pair of black boxers that leave nothing about his size to the imagination. Even not erect, he has plenty to show off.

"I came to get a glass of water and got distracted. It's so beautiful." But I'm studying the tattoos on his chest, not the serene ocean. If he could stand in the sea, preferably naked and wet, that would be the ideal view for me.

"Just looking out the window?" he echoes sceptically. "If I check for your phone, it'll still be there?"

I shrug. "Unless you moved it."

The control required to keep myself from twitching as he reaches up—he's ridiculously tall so it only needs him to stretch up an arm.

He feels for the phone, and when he finds it, surprise flits across his face. Our eyes meet.

"Good girl."

And even though I know it's not true, I can't help but respond, heating everywhere despite the air conditioning.

"Breakfast." He nods. "How do you take your coffee, moya lisichka?"

14

FELIKS

The sun rises, pink and creamy-yellow as we drink coffee and eat breakfast. She likes her coffee like her soul, nearly all white milk and sugar and froth. I slice mango, papaya, and pineapple for her, and she eats it all greedily, seeming to remember that neither of us have eaten properly since yesterday on the plane.

She stares longingly at the sea through the window. Maybe she's a mermaid, not a little fox.

"Swim," I tell her, though her brow furrows when I say I need to sort some things, so I won't join her.

"Not worried I might escape?"

I smile. "I'll catch you if you try."

I set up in a chair in the shade, with a good view of the beach, and start dealing with the small crises that crop up for any organisation that turns over more than a billion a year. You'd think that being a mafia boss, I'd be able to avoid this *gavno*, but apparently not.

It's earlier in the day here than back in London, so when I call my second-in-command I'm expecting news that he's found Ivan.

"Still waiting for information to come in," Evgeni says apologetically. "And there's a stupid problem with the marriage."

"Go on." This sounds like the sort of bullshit I don't want to deal with.

But I look out at the ocean, and while it usually calms me, the small head of Payton in the water somehow settles me even more.

"The marriage licence for the couple is in their names, with the location of your island. But they've decided not to get married. Apparently without the luxury wedding she didn't want the role of wife."

"I did him a favour," I mutter. "This doesn't sound like a problem."

"The licence has to be issued through Beckenham, and submitted to the central London registry. Technically it's already been issued, and the location is unchangeable. So they have the right to go to the island anytime, and get married. Or they can re-assign the licence to another couple."

Great. Fucking bureaucracy, and Ivan, that mudak, have turned my private haven into a wedding destination.

Payton is pushing her luck, of course, swimming a little around the bay, so I move along the beach to a position where I can see her again, although the house is out of sight. When our gazes meet, I know she's aware of what I'm doing. Keeping tabs on her.

"I've tried to hack into the central database, but I can't remove the listing. Only alter it." The apology in Evgeni's voice says he knows how furious I'm going to be.

But I'm not.

I'm just watching Payton. She's a drug, and brings the

sort of clarity I normally only achieve with several hours in the gym. For a moment, there's nothing, then a solution bubbles up.

"You can change the names?" It would be crazy. I look at the sand, hoping to ground myself.

"Yes." Evgeni's shrug is audible. "But how does that help?"

"Change them to Love, Payton, and…" I pause. I'm really doing this, aren't I? I push the warm sand with my toes. She'll hate me. "Rykov…"

"Ivan. Make her a wealthy widow." He thinks he follows my logic. "I'll—"

"Feliks." My mouth is dry. Ivan would be a smart way to solve this problem. But the idea of Ivan's name forever with Payton's is unbearable.

And Payton would be my perfect wife.

"Pakhan?" His shock is a wave down the phone line.

"Feliks Rykov and Payton Love."

Mine. She's mine. That's the only thought I can hold in my head.

"Okay," Evgeni says dubiously.

And if anyone is getting married on my island, it's me. "Do it now."

"Da." There's a pause and the sound of keyboard taps. "It's done."

"Good. What's the status of anything we're working on which is damaging to the London Mafia Syndicate?"

If Evgeni is confused by this second bizarre request, he has the sense to keep it to himself, and merely begins to reel off project names.

We discuss the risks of each one, given I have created what might be considerable tension with Richmond. It takes a while, with distractions for various other problems, but I'm satisfied that I'm not antagonising them more than is usual. We're on the last few issues, when Evgeni stops, mid-sentence.

"Pakhan, a report has just arrived. We know where Ivan is."

"Where?" I demand. "How quickly can you secure him?"

"Greenwich."

There's static in my brain for a second.

"He went there yesterday, and he hasn't returned. Neither have his friends."

That's not good. I'm not a man who's scared of much, but Greenwich is not someone I'd mess around with. He runs The Lazy Bean cafes that are dotted all through London—even some in my territory—and his reach is considerable. And although he's Bratva, he's a core part of the London Mafia Syndicate.

"Is Ivan dead?" I ask bluntly. That would save me a job.

"I don't know, Pakhan, we don't have…"

I look over at the water for my fix of Payton, and frown.

She's gone. I scan the sea, my heart in my throat.

Evgeni is saying something, but I've stopped caring. All I can see is that Payton isn't there and fuck. Fuck!

Has she drowned? Is she in trouble? Where is she?

"I'll call you back," I say, shoving my phone into my pocket as I start running to the water, my blood pumping desperately.

The horror of anything having happened to her is ice in my veins, despite the sun rising warm overhead, promising a beautiful day. I sprint to where the waves lap the shore, and stare at the sea. She's not there. She can't have gone past me, but she could have doubled back and swum the opposite way? I pray that my guess is correct, and that I can find her, setting off at a sprint back towards the house, feet slapping on the wet sand.

"Hey, sorry I didn't answer."

Spray arcs up as I slide to a halt at the sound of Payton's hushed voice from inside the house and relief crashes over me. I catch myself and change direction, heading across the beach, my pulse not getting the message that there aren't any monsters I need to slay to save her, or threat to pull her away from.

I glare at her back, stalking towards the open door. She's speaking on the phone.

Moya lisichka. She will be the death of me.

"Sorry you didn't answer?!" A girl who can only be Payton's sister Hayley yells from the video on Payton's phone. "Why didn't you call me as soon as you could?"

"I couldn't!" Payton glances to the side. "Look, I shouldn't even be talking to you now, but I heard my phone ringing and ran out of the water."

"No, you shouldn't be using that phone," I say, scowling down at Payton, who peeks up at me. Our gazes meet, and chemistry sparks between us.

On the screen, a man puts an arm over Hayley's shoulders and growls, "Rykov. What the fuck?"

"Who's that?!" Payton demands. Her eyes go wide and dart around as though finally taking in Hayley's surroundings on the screen. The unfamiliar apartment and the intimacy of the pose.

Hayley gives the man a happy glance. "Uh, well, some things have happened."

He smirks back at her. It takes me second but I recognise Greenwich. What the hell?

"Are you okay?" Payton says worriedly. My sweet girl is concerned about her sister. "I thought you were safe at home."

"Yeah. Safe." Hayley slants an eyebrow at Payton. "Your boyfriend tried to kill me, you know? A heads up would have been nice."

"I told you so," I say, my arms folded. This is why I kept Payton with me. Safe.

"Oh no." Payton covers her mouth, but her eyes are distraught. "I'm so sorry."

"I dealt with it," the man interjects mildly.

"What do you mean?" I grab the phone and hold it close to my face, scowling.

He turns so the screen is filled by him, trying to look tough. "Bring Payton back," Greenwich grits out. "And we'll talk about your son."

Talk? That's a euphemism if ever I heard one. Evgeni

said Ivan and his friends hadn't returned from Greenwich, and suddenly everything slots into place.

"Understood."

"So you'll return Payton—" Hayley begins.

"Nyet. She's *mine*," I snap and hang up.

15

PAYTON

He looks me up and down, and huffs out a furious breath. The phone clatters to the floor.

My sister is okay, and she knows I'm fine too. The weight from my shoulders is wonderful, but that's all mixed up with my gut churning. Feliks said I was his, and I went against his express instructions.

I'm not his good girl.

The silence between us is unbearable. A ticking bomb before it explodes.

"Sorry," I mutter eventually.

His brows lower even further, and if a man can have an internal battle raging inside of him, that's Feliks right now.

"You will be," he snarls, and it's a lightning strike, burning down my spine.

Jaw clenched, he seizes my hand and drags me with him into the bedroom. Fear squeezes my throat as I look up at Feliks' eyes, which have gone as wild as a winter storm at sea.

Abruptly, he drops my hand and strips off his shorts. I go bug-eyed.

"Put the white dress on," he snaps as he pulls on a pair of pale tan linen trousers.

"What?" I ask stupidly.

"White. Dress. Now." His tone has me scrambling to obey.

By the time I've managed to get it over my head, my hands shaking, Feliks is wearing a white shirt open at the collar, a tan suit, and shoes, and is watching me impatiently, no sign of humour or affection on his face.

The next thing I know, he's lifted and tossed me over his shoulder.

"Feliks!" I yell. Well. Squeal.

He makes for the front door we entered through, and I uselessly wriggle. His arm is braced tight over my thighs, and my chest is draped over his strong back. I'm hit by the fresh warm air as we leave the air-conditioned house, the door slamming behind us.

"Feliks, what are you doing?" I ask, propping myself up with my hands on his buttocks. He does have an exceptional bottom, even if he's a grumpy kidnapper.

He doesn't answer, but I recognise the path we took when he drove us from the jetty and distress crowds my mind. Is he getting rid of me? Taking me somewhere else? What does "mine" really mean?

But instead of going to the old pickup or continuing that direction on foot, he takes a smaller track.

"Feliks?" I try again, but he still refuses to reply. "I'm so sorry, but I had to talk to my sister. She'll have been beside herself."

"I know," he says abruptly.

That's good, I guess?

"So, why don't you put me down?"

He doesn't reply, and I crane my neck to look around at

where we're going. Moments later, we're through the trees and the path opens out to another beach, maybe even more beautiful than the one at the beach house.

In the middle of the sand there's a wooden arch covered in flowers and draped white fabric. I gape as Feliks strides over to it, stopping abruptly underneath.

He slides me down his body, rucking up the long dress I'm wearing, but I can feel every part of him, hard, on all my soft curves. Including the hardness between his legs that presses into me.

By the time my bare feet touch the sand, I'm hot everywhere, and squirming.

Feliks still doesn't say anything, but he takes a step away, a bit reluctantly, as though being out of arm's reach is as painful for him as it is for me.

Strange thought. This man feels as essential to me as air, water, my sisters, and my eReader.

I take in our surroundings. The flower-covered arch, the lines of floaty white fabric. White dress. Linen suit. Gorgeous, romantic setting.

My brain can't process it, because the pieces together are even more baffling. "Was this set up for that couple's wedding?"

He nods, his face lined with tension.

I look up into his face. "I don't understand."

"Yes, you do," he says harshly. "You're a smart girl. You know that I meant it."

Mine.

Recognition flashes between us. I can hardly dare to think what he seems to be saying. Us. Getting married.

A breeze catches my mostly-dry hair, and tugs at a lock, but before I can I push it out of my eyes, Feliks has stroked his fingers down the side of my face and tucked the unruly wisp behind my ear.

"That conversation started a ticking clock, Payton. Greenwich, the man your sister was with, is part of the London Mafia Syndicate. So is Richmond, the kingpin of the area you live in. And if they turn up here and try to take you from me, I'll kill them. It might be days until they arrive, but probably it'll be hours." He takes a deep breath. "If you're my wife, we might be able to avoid bloodshed. Maybe they'll respect that, and I won't be forced to protect what's *mine*."

My mouth has fallen open. I'm gaping like a very specific land-dwelling, Bratva boss-loving fish.

Loving?

Wait. What?

Can I love him after less than twenty-four hours? That's insane, isn't it?

Or fate, whispers my heart. He feels like the protective shell I should always have had. Not a fish after all, but a hermit crab that has spent its life naked, finally crawling into an iridescent shell with room to grow.

He's totally different to me. Hard and difficult and morally grey at best.

But we fit. More than any person I've ever met, Feliks is a balance to me.

I know what love is. I love my sisters, and in the space of less than a day, Feliks is like that, but with a sexy extra, and a depth of affection that scares me.

"We get married to ensure they don't try to take me from you, and then you won't kill them," I say.

"If there's one thing I've heard about the London Mafia Syndicate, it's that they value marriage." He takes my hand.

Interlacing our fingers, he swipes his thumb over my palm, then possessively over my knuckles.

And my god, he's never looked as attractive as he does right now. Sincere and potent and yet a bit vulnerable.

"If you really want to leave, I'll…" He stops, as though he can't bring himself to say more. "But if you'll stay with me, be my wife. Those are the options, and you need to decide quickly, because they'll be on their way. Accept that I'll kill them, or be my wife."

His wife. I want that from the bottom of my soul, but he's forgotten about all the other non-mafia issues. "What about Ivan?"

Feliks looks away, his brow creasing. "He's dead."

"But the man Hayley was with—"

"Probably killed him," Feliks interjects.

That blasts through me, but it's a wind at sea, sweeping everything clean. All that remains is relief that Feliks doesn't have to bloody his hands with his son's end, and Ivan won't come after Hayley or me again. I'll never have to pretend to like him.

There's just one question left. One thing between me and throwing myself into foolish but hopeful marriage with this gruff, grumpy, kind man who I'm besotted with. Maybe more.

"What about love?"

16

FELIKS

I knew this was inevitable, but where love is as familiar to Payton as her literal own name, I'm an infant, unschooled in this.

I stare at her. So small, so sweet. The thought of giving her up is enough to make me want to burn and smash and roar.

She wants me to tell her I love her. Even I, emotionally incompetent man that I am, can see that.

Terror grips my throat.

I can't say it.

Love? What do I know of it? What do I understand of that tender feeling when my whole life has been brutal choices and hard knocks? I'm as unprepared as a lion is for a gun fight.

"I told you not to ask questions you do not want the answer to, lisichka," I echo my warning from the plane.

"Do you love me?" Those big blue eyes regard me earnestly.

It works as well now as it did then. I sigh.

How is it that I'm wealthy and successful, but utterly

incompetent with the one thing I've just discovered means the most to me? Payton.

I try. I lick my lips, and will the words to emerge.

They don't.

Even though I've told thousands of lies, and done unspeakable things, I can't deceive this girl.

Saying the words is impossible.

But her face is crumpling, and fuck, no. I can't lose her now. I have to say *something*.

An explanation.

For a second I choke, then it's there, an involuntary spasm straight from my chest.

"I've never felt anything like what I feel for you, Payton." My voice is raw rasp, but it halts the fall of her expression into disappointment. "I don't have a ring to give you, and this wedding is..." I circle my hand to encompass the lack of guests or the usual marriage essentials. "I kidnapped you, and I haven't done any of this the right way, in fact I've fucked it up. But if you're my wife, I will give you a ring, and myself, and anything you want that I can buy, steal, sweat over, or extort. There aren't limits to what I'd do to make you happy. After knowing you, even for this brief time, kissing you, feeling you come on my tongue, and hearing you laugh, I'll die without you. I've lived forty-four years in the dark, and one day in the light, with you. I can't go back. The moment I saw you, I knew you were it for me."

Her mouth hangs open, but she doesn't reply, except to step closer to me, and sharp, silky hope flows into my chest. I grip her knuckles tighter.

"People say 'I'd die for her', and of course I would. But I'll do something much harder, if you'll let me. I'd die without you, but I'll live *for you*. There won't be a moment of my life that I'm not making your comfort and happiness my priority. You want me to be a better man? I'd do it. You want to live here, and never return to London? Absolutely. A dozen children? I'll dote on every single one. My future is in your hands. Every penny of my fortune, of billions, is yours. Every part of my ruined soul I lay at your feet."

Her other hand comes to rest on the lapels of my jacket.

"I don't know what love is," I confess, rawly. "But if it's that, then yes." I've been in mafia knife fights that were less terrifying than saying this. "And if you want me, then no force on earth, natural or manmade, or even the fucking London Mafia Syndicate, will keep me from marrying you today, and spending every day from now on protecting you and any family you'd bless us with."

There's a stunned silence, and the effort of not scooping Payton into my arms is an ache.

But there are stars in her eyes as she gazes up at me, and her lips tug upwards into a rueful smile. "You could just have said yes?"

Disbelief makes me light-headed. It was enough?

She hasn't left. Yet. She hasn't said no.

"That wouldn't have been the truth, and you deserve the truth."

She doesn't reply, and I take her hand from my chest, and bring it to my lips, kissing her knuckles one by one, my heart vibrating against my ribcage, as I wait for her to speak.

"Don't we need an officiant? Will it be legal?" she asks tentatively.

I quirk one eyebrow. "I own this island. I control Beckenham. It's legal if I say it is."

There's still a knot in my chest, because I can't force her to do this, and the excuse about the London Mafia Syndicate is just that. Even married, I might have to use the island's defences, because I won't give up Payton without a fight.

"Well, do you know the words for a wedding ceremony?"

My chest eases slightly. Does that mean she's considering marrying me?

"I don't go to many weddings," I confess.

"Not many invites for a mafia boss? Me neither. This is actually the first I've been to."

"Let's make it special then." I tug her hand so she's toe to toe with me, and yes. That's what I need. "I think there's 'I do'?"

"And other promises. Like..." She narrows her eyes. "Love, honour, and cherish."

"I will do whatever it takes, Payton." I lose myself in her blue eyes. *I'll try to love you, even though I don't know how, or even if I can feel that emotion*, I tell her silently. "I will honour every promise I make to you. I will obey the dictates of my heart to protect you from harm. Anything that happens, I'll be there, a buffer between you and everything that tries to steal your joy. You're my reason for living. I didn't know I was waiting for you. I didn't know I bought this island to see your eyes sparkle in blue that matches the pale water."

"And yours match the dark-blue water," she adds. "In sickness and in health, for richer, for poorer?"

"Yes. Though I'll do anything to prevent that. You're good at this." I can't help but smile back when she grins.

"Saw it in a movie."

"One of many reasons I need you." I grip her fingers even tighter, and bring my other hand to cup her cheek. "To keep me up to date on culture."

She giggles at that. "I don't think 'culture' is what most people would call my romcom films and smutty books."

"I promise to maim or kill, whichever you prefer, anyone who insults your taste in books."

Blushing and laughing, she turns her face into my hand to kiss my palm. But when she looks back up at me, her expression has sobered.

"What about kids?"

"I'll give you as many as you'd like," I admit, my throat sandpaper. "More than that. I'd be delighted to fill you up, over and over. But I'll care for our children properly. I won't miss any part of their lives."

"I'd like that," she breathes. "Do you really want to be a father, and my husband?

"I do. Do you want to be my wife?"

"I do."

There's a long moment when we just gaze at each other, the morning sun on the sides of our faces, and the wash of little waves on the shore.

It's as though something between us has clicked and locked in with those words.

"Is that it? Are you my husband now?"

"My wife," I growl, and gather her to me, picking her up by the bottom so her face is level with mine, pressing a kiss to her lips and she throws her arms around my neck. My cock, already half-hard, rises to the occasion. Her legs dangle down and she's just so much softness pressed to me.

I plunder her mouth with this kiss. I don't hold back. I can't hold her tight enough, or get her as close as I crave.

I need to be inside her. Breed my beautiful wife with all the babies she desires.

I spin us around to begin walking back to the house and

begin exactly that when she squeaks and giggles. Pulling back from the kiss, I look into her eyes.

"You like being spun, moya lisichka?"

She nods, joyful and a bit shy, almost embarrassed.

I take a few quick steps, and the sound of her laughter, and her clinging to me makes my heart ready to float away, so I do it more, spinning her around in my arms until her feet are flying out and we're both grinning at each other.

My heart is full to bursting. She's mine. She's my wife, in the way that counts—between us—even if we might have to do some legal and public stuff when we get back to London.

I just want to squeeze her so tightly she's attached to me always.

Then she gets her lips on mine and we're kissing as I spin her.

"My perfect girl," I say as I eventually bring us to a dizzy halt. We cling to each other even once I've lowered her to the sand. "You make me so happy. I had no idea I could feel like this."

"Phsshh." She glances away, cheeks heating.

"It's true." I bend and pick her back up, this time in a bridal carry, her knees lying over my elbow. But she still has her hands linked around my neck.

The soft, white sand gives way to the crunch of gravel, and she snuggles into me.

"What now?" she asks as we reach the beach house.

"My sweet wife." I allow her to slide down my chest a little, so my rock-solid erection pokes at her arse. "I think you know what I want to do."

She presses her lips together, eyes sparkling as I elbow my way into the cool of the house, toeing off my shoes, kicking the door closed, and carrying her to our bedroom.

I toss her onto the bed, and she bounces with a squeak of surprise. Then I'm stripping off my clothes, buttons popping in my haste.

I'm desperate to be inside her.

"Are we going to consummate our marriage?" Her eyes are wide at my big, naked body.

I crawl over her and grab one of her hands as it comes up to touch my chest.

"In a way. I'm going to get you so wet you'll be embarrassed by how soaking you are between the legs, make you come on my tongue until you're wrecked." I roll my hips, pressing my erection against her soft body. "Then I'll break your little cunt open with my big cock and fuck you until I unload my balls right up against your womb, to get you pregnant. I'll make you *mine*."

17

PAYTON

Wet heat gushes between my legs at his filthy words.

My husband should be less intimidating naked, but he's not. A cock that large, red, veined, and throbbing, is practically a weapon. His tattoos continue down his body, over his hips and thighs and I want to trace every single one. But since he's on top of me, there are more urgent matters.

Feliks doesn't ask or go slow.

"Forgive me," he says abruptly, then rears up, grabs the middle of my delicate white dress in both hands, and tears it open.

He groans as my bikini is revealed.

I'm motionless in what I suppose should be horror, as the same violence is done to the string bikini that I've been bonding with this past day, his tattooed knuckles brushing my skin.

The sound of the rips and snaps is brutal in the hushed room, and I fight the urge to cover myself, suddenly shy.

Tattered fabric is strewn over my body and around, but Feliks doesn't seem to care, because I'm revealed enough. My breasts are naked, and he lets out a feral grunt as he lowers himself to touch his mouth to my chest, kissing over my bare shoulders and then down to my nipples with a fierce intensity.

"I've wanted to worship these since I saw you in that bikini," he says hoarsely, his lips not moving from my skin. "You're so fucking beautiful, it's unreal. And you belong to me. I'm the luckiest fucker alive."

Then he's shifted and has his mouth on one of my pebbled nipples and his fingers on the other. The graze of his teeth is a sign he's not playing. I gasp as the mixture of pleasure with a slice of pain rips down me from my breasts to my clit. "Oh!"

"Yes," he rasps, and tweaks my nipple, making me gasp.

I writhe against him, needing him closer. He has his hard-on pressed over my pussy, and his weight on me is arousing in a way I didn't expect.

He's effortlessly holding me in place with his big body and the sheer power of him makes my clit pulse as he licks and nibbles me. It takes no time at all for me to be a panting mess, shimmering with desire for him.

"Feliks, please." I plunge my fingers into his silver and black hair and try to urge him... I don't know where. Up so we're face to face? Closer to my breasts to have those insanely pleasurable trades?

He groans as he drags away my ruined bikini bottoms.

"You're so beautiful. Fuck, you're absolutely gorgeous, the most perfect thing I've ever seen. Look at your little body, so sweet and curvy and delicate."

But he makes a different choice, chuckling to himself as he ducks his head between my legs, and my face is flaming.

"Feliks! What are you doing?" I thought he would take my virginity?

He looks up, and his expression is pure sin. Dark-blue eyes gleaming.

"Exactly what I said. Getting you ready to have my cock in your virgin pussy, and be loved by me. I have to make you feel good. I need to taste you, and have you quake beneath me as you come."

He doesn't give me a chance to react, impatiently pushes my knees further apart, tossing my thighs over his shoulders, and dives his head back down.

There are no slow and respectful touches now. Not like when he was covering me with sunscreen. His mouth finds my core immediately and sucks.

I scream. He yanks pleasure from me so powerful it's a shock that leaves me gripping at Feliks' scalp for dear life.

His shoulders rock as he laughs and does it again, and it's only when he braces his arm over my hips that I realise I've jerked with his touch, my body responding without my say-so.

"You're going to take it, lisichka," he murmurs before holding me down even harder and bringing his mouth to my pussy.

I hardly know what happens then. There's only Feliks' lips and tongue and his arms keeping me exactly where he wants me, and the fastest build towards climax that I've ever had. His fingers leave where he's caressing my thigh soothingly, and nudge at my entrance as he licks my clit relentlessly. The first finger is slight discomfort that turns into utter bliss. The next is a pinch and a fullness. Then he does something with his fingers, a thrust that makes me feel I'm his to command, and he just told me to come, because he pairs the movement with an insistent suck on my clit, and I explode.

My orgasm racks through me like white light, sparks

illuminate me from the inside where he's penetrated me right down to my toes. It pulses down my legs and up my chest, Feliks rumbling and not letting up, drawing more and more from me.

Then as fast as it happened, it's sliding away, leaving me boneless.

"Perfect, that was perfect. Such a good girl." He praises me in a low voice, and it's only when his breath makes all the fine hairs around my ear stand up that I realise I've closed my eyes. I open them to find him over me, a satisfied expression on his face.

And a lot of shiny juices. Mine, from him hungrily sucking my clit.

"You did that beautifully," he says hoarsely. "Can you be a good girl for me now and take my whole cock?"

I'm destroyed, but ensnared again by his navy eyes. He rocks his hips and we both moan as the silk-over-hot-steel tip of his erection notches at my entrance.

Despite having come, I'm flooded with a passionate need for more.

"Spread your thighs as wide and high as you can. Let me into the secret heaven you kept intact for me. I'm going to break you in the best way, and remake you as mine."

My hands are on his shoulders, and he's just so gorgeous. I want him, but he hasn't moved to do as he has threatened. So I slide my palms down his torso and he hisses as I reach the place where the length of his erection is resting at my needy hole.

I encircle his cock with my fingers, and he lets out a shuddering breath that sounds like he's trying to keep control. I explore, and he groans. And when I drop my hand to the sack of his balls, he makes an involuntary twitch, sliding into me and I gasp at the flare of pain.

"No, no, no." One second, he's on his elbows above me, his weight held, the next he's pressing me into the mattress with his body and has got both my hands in his. He brings them ruthlessly above my head, pinning my wrists with one hand. "I can't keep control of myself if you're doing things to drive me wild. Be a good girl for me."

He eases back and despite the removal of that pinch, I miss him.

I writhe as his solid, hair-dusted chest presses to my hard nipples. The bulk of him is unexpectedly hot holding me prisoner. And with my arms above my head, I'm so vulnerable. Spread. My legs are as open as he demanded, and I'm entirely unable to move.

I love it.

"Yes." His eyes go serious, as he shifts his weight back onto his arm and I almost grumble at the change. "That's better. I want to feel every second as I take you."

Then he presses his lips to mine in a passionate, possessive kiss, and rocks his hips forwards and into me, breaching me with infinite slowness. The sharp pain is brief this time, and as he pushes in further, it dulls, then something gives inside me, and my inner walls throb with bliss. It feels like he's too big, but with gradual but insistent movements, he forces me to accept him, swallowing my whines with kisses.

"See?" he says against my lips. "It's better when you let me take care of you."

I haven't got words to reply. I'm just his creature, with a mix of pain and pleasure and fullness buzzing in my blood.

I whimper, loving the sensation of being totally caught by him. Owned.

"Such a good girl," he growls. "You're sloppy-wet for me, aren't you?"

He withdraws a tiny bit, then goes another inch deeper,

and part of me thinks that's the limit. But he's right. I'm soaked, and despite the shot of discomfort, he advances again.

"Your tight little cunt feels amazing, lisichka. Go on." He pushes. "Take more."

As though I have a choice. But that's overrated. What he's giving is even better. Being remade by his massive cock is everything I didn't know I wanted.

"Husband." I roll my hips, trying to get him in some unknown place inside of me that feels incredible. "Please."

His face lights up. "My wife."

I hook my feet around his waist and let out a breathy, needy sound as he slides all the way home. Inside me, his hips flush with mine. He steals my breath with how he's stretched me and filled me with himself. It's as though I can feel him in my lungs. Up to my heart.

He hasn't exactly said that he loves me, but as he brushes his lips over mine, and whispers, "Ready?" I know it. I'm overwhelmed by the emotion between us.

I nod and he pulls away a tiny bit and pushes back in, and the sparks from where we join are pure pleasure. There's no pain now. Just the magic of being joined with this man.

"Fuck, you're so tight. You're mine now." He wraps a tendril of my hair that's next to his hand around his finger and gently tugs. "I own you, to care for and fuck and worship. My wife."

That shouldn't turn me on.

He draws out nearly all the way, then plunges back into me, and I let out a strangled sound. He does it again, and each time the seam of the head of his cock does something magical, sending flares of pure ecstasy out from where we're joined. The push of him inside me, buried as deep as he'll go and the base of his cock stretching me out, is even better. A low, throbbing pleasure that's the mirror of how good it feels when the crown is at my entrance.

I'm weak with it, babbling, straining my thighs further apart and that's even more intense. The alternating slide, thrust right into me, then teases to the sensitive place where he's almost pulled out is mind-bending. I've never felt anything like it.

I dig my heels into the top of Feliks' muscled thighs, urging him on.

And he obeys. He gradually goes faster and harder, and I'm pinned, overwhelmed by his cock ramming into my pussy.

His stormy dark gaze bores into me, as though that's all the stimulation he requires, as he takes me rhythmically, his fingers moving to my clit and I crumple, unable to do anything but whine in pure desire as he both uses my body for his own satisfaction, and provides everything I need. He's controlling this, making me crazy for him.

It's addictive already.

I've never had sex before, but I know that this is something special. Unique.

We were made to fit together this way.

18

FELIKS

Her body is my custom-made heaven. Hot, wet, tight. But so much more. There's magic between us as I thrust, careful of my virgin girl. This feels like nothing I've ever experienced. I'm holding her down, yes, but she angles her hips to meet my every move.

However good I imagined Payton would feel when she submitted to me, this is better.

I still have her hands trapped above her head, held with one of mine, and my core muscles are screaming at me as I thrust, holding myself one handed, careful not to put pressure on her wrists, and stroke the slippery bud of her clit. My belly connects with hers every time I bottom out in her sopping pussy, our flesh slapping together.

"Payton." Her name is my prayer.

It's raw and meaningful as we alternate between staring into each other's eyes, and when that's too much, I bring my mouth down onto hers, kissing her ravenously.

My balls pull up, and the savage bliss of her threatens to shove me into orgasm. But she has to come on my cock first.

I need to feel her pleasure as she clenches around my length more than I need air.

Her breathing changes as I circle her clit more insistently, interspersing long, slow strokes of my whole length into her with short, shallow thrusts that focus the swollen tip of my erection on her sensitive entrance. She keens and tightens. I lift my head to see her face.

"Come for me," I rasp.

And she does. Brutal pride envelops me as she grips my cock.

"Feliks!" she sobs out my name as she comes in waves that almost cause me to black out as I hold myself back, just giving her the continued friction to prolong her orgasm.

It's all I can do to stop myself from following. I release her hands and roll us over to ease the temptation to rut into her. She's liquid over me as I arch my hips up into her far slower than my cock demands, the sound of each thrust into her soaked pussy absolutely filthy.

"Being covered by you is the best thing." I wrap my arms around her and skim my fingers down her back, up to her silky hair and down to her soft little bottom. "I want you to be my wife, my slut, my whore, my goddess. Everything to me." I pour out the words in broken shards into her ear as she lies on my chest. "All that I've ever dreamed of wanting. A dozen things I didn't know I needed. I swear I'm going to have you dripping with my seed every day until you're pregnant with my baby. And then I'll probably have to have you twice as often, because imagining you pregnant makes me so hard I might burst out of my skin."

"Feliks," she murmurs, then rubs her cheek on my shoulder like a cat scenting me, and pushes up onto her arms, hands on my pectorals.

"I've ruined your tiny cunt with my fat dick, haven't I?" My voice is scratchy. "And you'll love it."

"Yes, yes."

We both moan as the angle of my cock inside her shifts, and she adjusts her thighs on either side of my waist, figuring out how to get stable enough to move over me, experimenting.

I lie back and run my hands up her sides, cupping her breasts and squeezing her nipples. I groan as I explore her body, utterly disbelieving that she's here. She's mine.

Emotion bubbles up in my chest as she rides me, using my cock with more confidence by the second. This is the culmination of all the feelings she's inspired from the moment I first saw her.

All those things I said I do for her, and that's just the start. I'd do anything. I'd risk everything.

I love her.

It's quietly in my head at first, tentative. This feeling is alien. It's been years since I've had sex, decades since I've cared, and forever since I loved. I don't think I've ever loved anyone. Not fully, with my entire body and soul.

It's a beat, as I hold her waist and bring her down on my cock when she tires.

The words are insistent.

I love you.

I love you.

"Ya tebya lyublyu." I've said it in Russian before my brain understands, and while I half expect there to be cracks of thunder, and fireballs raining from the sky, instead there's just the slightly confused and hazy-eyed with pleasure girl on top of me, unaware I've split open my ribcage and offered her my bleeding, beating heart.

And it's good. It's amazing, like the best high I've felt. I'm free.

I say it again in Russian, and bring my hand to her neck, holding her as she bounces on my cock. Mine. I love you.

"I love you."

She stops instantly, eyes wide, as shocked as I am.

Then I've gathered her in my arms and flipped her down onto her back, some primal part of my brain afraid she'll run from me now I've confessed this.

I withdraw and slam into her, trapping her with my body.

"I love you." My voice is hoarse. "I love you." There are no other words.

I'm taking her too hard and fast, and she's so hot and wet and tight that I'm barely restraining myself from shooting my load into her. Right up by her fertile young womb. But she's insane too, wrapping her legs and arms around me as best she can as I pound her into the bed, too crazed to be gentle, too in love to do anything but give myself over to the overwhelming sensation of us together.

This time I have to cram my hand between us. I can't make space, I have to be inside her as deeply as possible. But it's enough.

She breaks again, quicker but just as intense.

"*My* husband." She grips my hair tight and cries out as she comes.

That possessiveness makes me feral. I slam into her, out of control, my face screwed up and an animalistic roar blasting from my chest as my orgasm explodes from the base of my spine, up my shaft in a wave of ecstasy that sweeps through me, washing out all the bleak loneliness and leaving only her.

Payton. My wife. The woman I love and will give anything.

I'm weak as the pleasure rolls over me, all my strength nothing. I'm unable to hold myself off my girl. All my muscles break as my orgasm blasts through me.

I collapse and roll to the side, bringing Payton with me.

And as I wrap my arms around her and pant and shudder with intensity of what just occurred, I hear words I never even dreamed of.

"I love you, too."

19

PAYTON

I've never felt so content in my life. My body is buzzing from head to toe, and it sounds ridiculous, but I can still feel Feliks inside me. Or the echo of him. My inner passage feels as though it has been massaged, and the whole area between my legs is humming.

My head is clear, and every time a worry creeps forwards to intrude, the sated pleasure of how good he's made me feel acts as a defensive shield.

I'm lying half over Feliks' chest, his strong arms around me, the steady thud of his heart beneath my cheek, and his solid thigh between mine. He's breathing evenly, and running the fingers of one hand through my hair.

"My wife," he murmurs eventually, the sound going through my body as much as into my ears. "I love you." Then he repeats words in Russian, pressing a kiss to my forehead.

He squeezes me tighter, and I try to press myself to him. I can't get close enough. Meeting him has been like magnets aligning. Feliks has snapped into place in my heart, and I don't think I could pull myself away from him. I certainly don't want to.

"I love you too." I smooth my hand over his pectoral muscle, then up and over his shoulder, where the snake glares at me. He makes a low, purring noise, and I marvel at the way I can touch him. He's mine.

"You have a lot of tattoos." I want to memorise them. Know them all.

"Yes. I think I'm missing a little fox," he replies with amusement. "I might see if I can have one across my chest where you are now, that runs over all the others, like you have in my life."

"You'll get a fox tattoo?" I lift my head to look fully into his face. I'm absurdly pleased.

"Of course." He cups the nape of my neck in a possessive gesture that floods me with yet more arousal, despite everything we've already done. "I have a new tattoo when something important happens."

"They're like achievement stickers," I joke to disguise the fluttering in my tummy.

"Being a mafia boss is hard," he says dryly. "I deserve stickers."

"What about the snake?" It feels dangerous and daring to run my hand over the stark geometric lines of the snake's body as it curves around his bicep.

"Ah, yes." He sighs. "I thought I'd add a section to that, but it might be more than one, though not for the reason I imagined."

I tilt my head to the side, puzzled.

"You can see that the snake isn't complete?" He twists his arm to show me where it comes to an abrupt halt, without a tail. He traces a small rectangular part of the snake's body. "Each section represents a life I've taken."

His simple words grab me by the throat, because there are *a lot* of those twisting around his bicep.

I'm silent for a moment.

"Don't be too sad," he adds wryly. "That tattoo might represent death, but it's also life. Mostly, if I hadn't killed those men, they would have killed me."

"Then I'm glad," I say passionately. "I'm happy you did what you needed to so you're here with me."

Understanding passes between us.

"Maybe eventually I'll have the tail inked gradually darker with every year that goes by without me killing anyone."

"I'd like that."

We smile at each other. Then he increases the pressure on the back of my neck until I come, willingly, and kiss him, and he pulls me down fully on top of him, and I gasp as his erection digs into my thigh.

"Again?" I whisper against his lips. "I thought men needed—"

He rumbles a rueful laugh. "I just need *you*."

Later, after multiple orgasms and some very filthy words to accompany me taking Feliks in my mouth, and a luxurious meal for lunch because we're both ravenous, we return to the beach.

We splash in the sea, Feliks chasing me, me pretending to swim away and struggle, when all I want is to be with him.

I have my arms around his neck and we're kissing in the shallow water when a slight buzzing starts, at first almost imperceptible. Then louder, and my heart pounds as Feliks breaks our kiss to look out to sea, where a spec has appeared on the horizon.

A boat.

"What is it?"

"Trouble." He hoists me solidly into his arms as fear grips my throat. "And death."

20

FELIKS

I hoped we'd have more time as newlyweds before I had to kill people.

We wash off and dress quickly, and Payton trails me in a sundress she's thrown on, but I require more clothing for placement of weapons. A holster at my ankle and over my shoulder, then a suit jacket.

Slipping the guns into place gives all my years of experience a new focus. Payton.

"If I tell you to stay in the house, will you?" I ask her.

She looks at me like I'm mad. "No way."

"It would be the safest place for you. I'd really prefer it, because if anything happened to you, I'd..." There aren't words for how much it would crush me to see Payton hurt. And to live without her? Death. It would be death.

However, I'm not an idiot. It would be better for her to come with me than to be in more danger because she isn't where I expect.

"Please. Stay here. For me." It's not a command, it's a plea.

Biting her lip, she shakes her head. "My place is by your side, because what if they try to hurt you?"

I bark a laugh. "They're not going to harm me." The whole concept is ridiculous. "Come on." I hold out my hand. "They really don't know what they're walking into."

The proximity alarm for the jetty goes off on the panel by the front door and on my phone, showing a boat from the north that we saw, and another from the south. I open the app for my state-of-the-art defence system and check that the drones are in position, sending some to both boats. They pick up human targets and lock on immediately.

It's only a few minutes in the pickup then we're at the jetty. The boat comes in, one of the Mafia Syndicate is mooring up as Payton and I get out of the vehicle.

She cuddles into my side, and I sling my arm over her shoulders as we walk down to the water, my phone in my other hand ablaze with alerts. A group of men I recognise from various incidents in London step ashore.

"You're a long way from home, gentleman." My voice comes out as a territorial growl.

"Hayley!" Payton squeals.

"And lady." I dip my head. "Stay with me, moya lisichka," I murmur to Payton when I feel her twitch to go to her sister.

She stills obediently.

"Payton, are you alright?" Hayley, who looks like a slightly bigger, less beautiful copy of Payton, steps forward.

"We're here for the girl," Richmond says, revealing a pistol at his side. "Give her to us now, Beckenham, and no one needs to get hurt."

"Apologies for your wasted trip, but Payton is remaining with me," I reply with deceptive calm.

Greenwich steps up. "You're outnumbered."

"Don't come any closer, I'm warning you," I say mildly, glancing down at my phone screen. Greenwich and Richmond share a sideways glance.

"Payton, come to your sister," Richmond says.

My good girl doesn't move.

"One more step forward, and I'll be forced to protect what's mine," I warn.

"Look," Greenwich snarls and pulls out a gun.

I touch his image on the overhead view on my phone, and he lights up red. I choose the "scare" button, and confirm.

A hail of bullets rain from the sky a few feet to the side of Greenwich and he jumps aside, protectively pulling Hayley with him with a yelp.

"What the fuck, Beckenham?!" he bellows, as the other men go pale, and step away.

I sigh. "You think I have this island all to myself without defence?" I roll my eyes. "And call off your men at the south, or I'll be forced to deal with them more directly."

"What have you got there?" asks Harlsden, hands in his pockets. He glances up at the sky. "Drones and, like, a games console?"

"More or less," I confirm.

"Nice." He nods. "Good bit of kit."

"Fucking drones," complains Richmond looking up. "When did we start doing our business with toys? As bad as poison. Give me a proper shoot-out any day."

"You sound like an old man," says Harlsden.

Richmond grumbles, but pulls out a phone and issues an order to stand down.

"Are you okay?" Hayley says, and I growl as she starts to approach. She's shaking, and her voice is high with fear.

Payton gives me a cross little glance, and I press my mouth into a flat line.

Okay. No killing her sister.

"I could ask you the same thing," Payton replies. "Who are these men?"

"Maxim is..." Hayley blushes. "My new... Boyfriend? Things happened after Ivan attacked me."

"And he killed my son." Might as well take that moral high ground, since it'll help get rid of them.

"He—" Greenwich begins.

"And I appreciate you disposing of that problem for me," I add smoothly. I can't bring myself to feel more than token regret about Ivan's death when the result has been me finding Payton.

His eyebrows raise to a height only slightly lower than the drones hovering overhead. "You're welcome?"

"And thank you for letting me know in person, but I think it's time you left. I have a honeymoon to enjoy with my wife." I smile down at Payton.

"You really got married?" Hayley cries out, wringing her hands with concern.

"He kidnapped her," Richmond growls. "From my territory."

I meet Richmond's angry green eyes. Yeah, that might take a bit of smoothing over. Possibly some money.

"Payton, can we just talk for a moment?" Hayley takes a cautious step forwards, and Payton looks at her longingly.

I can't withhold anything from my girl. I check my app. The drones are still perfectly online, locked onto each of the men.

Bringing my hand to Payton's throat, I tilt her face up. Her trusting eyes meet mine. She's so beautiful. My instincts war inside me. But I love her, and I'm certain she belongs to me.

"Go to your sister." Then I release her, and her incandescent smile tells me I've done the right thing. The sisters are in each other's arms instantly.

I glare at the men behind them.

The two girls talk as fast as a machine gun, but so high-pitched I think I can't catch half of it because only dogs can hear that frequency.

"Do you think we should hire some girls in their early twenties as spies? No need to even encrypt. No one else has a hope of deciphering their speech," says Harlsden casually.

"Wait so..." Payton says, then the rest is impenetrable.

"My wife isn't in that business," I mutter. But he has a point.

Payton turns to me. "My sister is with your enemy?"

"Yes." I scowl. This could be inconvenient.

"But..." She pouts, then resumes talking to Hayley.

They're so similar in some ways, and clearly happy to be reunited, that I can't spoil it for Payton.

I was wondering, and I suppose this is what love is. Her pleasure is more important to me than my interests, or those of Beckenham.

"Perhaps we can come to some terms," I say warily, turning to the other men. Hopefully they won't need permission from all of the members, because I sold weapons to the Essex Cartel last year, and I don't doubt the London Mafia Syndicate is aware. They certainly will be when Essex uses them. And I did kill a few of Westminster's men only a few months ago, but they were in Beckenham trying to go behind my back and get support for a fucking pedestrianisation scheme, and how are the businesses in my area supposed to keep going without people being able to drive and park near the shops?

There's a tense silence, then Harlsden shrugs. "Why doesn't he join the London Maths Club?"

"He," Greenwich points at me angrily, "doesn't represent the ideals of the Maths Club. He *kidnapped* her. That's rule one. No kidnapping."

"More of a guideline, I think," Harlsden mutters.

"Kidnapping the woman you're going to marry is practically compulsory for the London Maths—" Richmond swears colourfully. "I mean, Mafia Syndicate."

"You people are entirely unserious," I say levelly. "Is it true you call it the Maths Club because someone couldn't admit to their wife that he was a mafia boss?"

"Yes, Canary Wharf. That—" Richmond begins.

"Serious enough to kill your son and all his friends." Greenwich folds his arms. "And I bet I could kill you before your drones took me out."

"You'd be dead before I hit the ground," I reply, and it's no more than the truth.

"You're not going to kill us, and we won't take the girl from you," Harlsden says tersely. "So could you call off your drones, Beckenham? And Greenwich, stop antagonising him."

Greenwich gives me a dark look, but mutters, "Fine."

"You're sure?" Hayley says as she steps back from Payton, drawing my attention, so I leave the drones.

Payton nods. "Absolutely." And her voice has that ring of certainty. She glances around at me.

We're all watching her now.

"Okay, we think you should all put your weapons away, and be friends, since we're sisters, and she loves him."

Payton points at Greenwich. "And I love you." She smiles sweetly at me.

Richmond looks as though he swallowed a parrot.

"How about they leave, and I won't kill—?" I suggest to Payton, who gives me puppy eyes.

"That only solves the immediate problem," Harlsden interrupts. "Once we're back in London, the full force of the London Maths Club—"

"You have to join their club," Hayley says, like this is easy.

Richmond groans and Greenwich shoves his hands in his pockets and looks up in resignation as though expecting heaven—or my drones—to strike him down.

"Do you want me to join the Maths Club?" I ask Payton.

Her gaze flicks between all the stern-jawed mafia men, then settles on me.

"Yes," she says clearly.

Okay, I'm helpless against that. This truly is love.

"The first of many things that are totally against my instincts that I will do for you, lisichka." I nod my head towards the pickup. "Fine. There are cold drinks in the fridge, and it's very hot out here."

"Oh good idea. Thank you!" Payton goes up on tiptoes to kiss my cheek, then grabs Hayley's arm and leads her off the jetty.

"Westminster is going to kill me when he finds I've let you into the Mafia Syndicate," Richmond grumbles. "You'd better behave yourself."

I bare my teeth in an approximation of a simile.

"Feliks, will you drive?" Payton calls from beside the pickup.

I pause, because if I don't have the controller in my

hands, the drones take longer to deploy. But I glance between my wife and her sister's partner, and the men who came to fetch and defend Payton.

Really, I have no quarrel with them so long as they don't touch Payton. With a sigh, I send the drones back to their bases, and close the app. "Let's get out of the sun before everyone turns into a beetroot."

With Payton and Hayley squashed into the passenger seat, and the rest of the visitors in the flat bed of the pickup, we're in the house and cracking open beer and soft drinks within ten minutes. Since I can't keep my hands off Payton, and Greenwich is Hayley's huge lumbering shadow, we end up all talking.

And I confess he's not a total idiot. Before long, there's a festive atmosphere, and snacks out, people sitting on the decking, and it's altogether not what I expected for a mafia get together, never mind a rescue attempt.

Greenwich shares an anecdote about his data collection from the cafes he runs, and given my business in drones, security software, and defence, it's annoying to find that not only is he a decent guy, I suspect we could do some work which would benefit us both.

He apologises again for Ivan and tells me how he killed him for threatening Hayley. I shrug. Shot through the head was better than my son deserved, and a quicker death than he'd have had from me.

Everyone has rolled up sleeves, has taken off their suit jackets, and two of the London Mafia Syndicate members are comparing guns, and debating the advantages of a printed custom weapon versus an old-school pistol. A shrill tone cuts through the voices, and I reach for my gun.

So does Greenwich, and it's only when Payton laughs that I pause.

"Thats' my phone!" In a second, she's found it from where I discarded it, and blinks at the screen. "It's the private investigator. Hello," she answers before I can say it might be a trap, or Hayley can finish the exclamation of surprise she's beginning. Then Payton's eyes go wide. "You've really found her?!"

"Oh my god. They've found Taylor?" Hayley gasps.

"Yes, yes. Hold on, I need to go somewhere quieter to talk," Payton says.

"I didn't even know Payton had a PI searching for Taylor," I hear Hayley explain to Greenwich as Payton takes the call onto the beach. I grab a pen and notepad and follow my wife, handing both to her.

She gives me a surprised look then a grateful smile, and I'm as warmed by providing for her and the appreciation that reflects back as the tropical sun.

"You know," she says as she puts the phone down several minutes later. "Indirectly, you paid to find Taylor."

Through my son giving her gifts, and her selling them.

"Your cleverness had two advantages. It brought us together, and it has found your sister." I put one finger beneath her chin and lift it to place a soft kiss on her forehead, then her lips. "Now let's go in and tell the others."

Everyone turns as we walk onto the deck.

"Well?" demands Greenwich.

"Taylor is with an exclusive, private ballet troupe—" Payton says.

"She's a soldier?" interrupts Harlsden.

"She's not a troop. Troupe is the word for a group of ballet dancers," I snap. "Under-educated idiot," I add under my breath.

"It's secretive, and the girls who dance are basically prisoners," Payton continues.

"Which is why she hasn't contacted us." Hayley's face is full of distress.

Greenwich pulls her into his chest, both facing forwards. "We'll go and get her."

"It's not that easy." I heard some of the conversation and read Payton's notes. "We'd need a contact to get a seat at a show, and the PI only has one. They're going back to Russia and doing a performance for the Volk Bratva."

Greenwich makes an injured sound.

"Who is that?" Payton asks me.

"A Bratva even I wasn't stupid enough to get involved with," I reply. "I wouldn't be welcome."

"Neither would I," says Greenwich, regretfully. "We'll just have to fight our way—"

"And risk Taylor getting caught in cross fire? Absolutely not," I interject.

"Surely we can—" Richmond begins.

"He's my old boss." We all fall silent as Harlsden swigs his beer casually. "The Pakhan of Volk," he clarifies unnecessarily. His rolled-up sleeves reveal a jagged, geometric wolf as he lowers his arm. The sign of the Volk Bratva. Greenwich and I see it at the same time, and exchange a look.

How did he get out alive?

"I'll go." Harlsden shrugs. "It'll be messy, but I have business that could plausibly take me there."

"This would be a suicide mission," Richmond says, scowling. "If they find out you're part of the London Mafia Syndicate, they'll string you up."

"Fun." Harlsden nods grimly. "I've been a bit bored recently."

Payton nibbles on her fingernail.

"I think it would be better if Greenwich and I—" I don't like the man. He's not trustworthy.

"No." Richmond steps forward. "This is my call because Taylor Love was last seen in my territory. And Harlsden is the best person to do this. We'll fund the trip."

"And I'll provide a bonus if you bring Taylor back safe," Greenwich says.

Harlsden rolls his eyes. "I have plenty of money."

"And untouched," I growl. I don't trust this svolach.

"Of course," Harlsden scoffs. "It's just getting one girl away from a dance group. It'll be fine."

I'm momentarily appeased. Then I look down at Payton, drawing her to me instinctively as she smiles up at me.

If Taylor is anything like her sister, Harlsden might find this mission more difficult than he expects.

EPILOGUE
PAYTON

Seven years later

This is heaven.

I'm sitting on the beach in the shade of a palm tree, with the latest released book from my favourite author. I'm six months pregnant with our fifth baby, and just getting to the "I think I'll stay out of the sun, with the occasional swim in the sea" stage of pregnancy, rather than running around I'd usually do.

Feliks is taking care of the children, and I've been looking forward to this book for months, so there's really no reason why I shouldn't be nose deep into it. The water is almost perfectly calm today, just a light breeze that cools and causes ripples. Ideal weather. But even when they're not asking for my attention, my family is distracting.

Okay, my husband especially.

I look out over to the floating raft where Feliks is with the kids. Six-year-old Ezra, five-year-old Kaia, four-year-old Asher, and our toddler, Nova. Asher and Nova have arm bands on. They're all too cute. Tanned and lean like their father, and as happy in the water as little otters.

Feliks checks in with each child in turn, and I wonder what they're doing. They're lined up on the edge of the raft.

"Three, two, one…" Feliks calls.

Oh, it's a race. Of course.

"Go!"

The kids jump and dive into the water, with varying degrees of elegance. The older two manage quite good dives, but our smallest girl hurls herself in with all the glee of a puppy, sending up a splash so big it even hits a laughing Feliks.

The kids all swim towards the beach, and I put my book away, because I can see where this is going, and I protect my books from excited children soaked with seawater.

I lean back in my chair and stroke my belly where Feliks' newest little printsessa is kicking, and smile contentedly as I watch the kids swim frantically.

Ezra is in the lead, but Kaia is close behind. Being the youngest, Nova is at the rear, but what she lacks in speed she makes up for in pure sass.

When Ezra reaches well over halfway, Feliks yells "I'm coming for you!" and dives gracefully into the water seeming to propel him half of the distance.

Then he's swimming after the now-shrieking and giggling kids. Watching Feliks is maybe even better when I'm not being chased by him. He has powerful arms and that tattooed bulky upper body is delicious in all situations, but especially when he's above me, pinning me with his weight and his cock and telling me I'm his good girl, or he's being adorable playing with our babies.

Feliks quickly catches Nova, and effortlessly grabs her, making an animal growling sound and Nova shrieks with delight. He picks her up with one arm and tows her with him as he continues to close the gap with the other kids. Asher is picked up next, but Ezra has already reached the shallows.

I smile as I remember my first play chase with Feliks, and blush a little as I think of the mini chase around the kitchen we had only a few nights ago.

But then I'm focused on Ezra as he sprints across the sand. Feliks wades in the shallow water, pausing to urge Kaia onto his back as he catches her, and scoops Nova and Asher up in his arms.

"Mummy! Yay!" Ezra throws himself into my waiting arms, sand and water flying everywhere, and I laugh.

"You won!" I hold up one hand for a high-five and his small hand smacks mine. He's so like his dad, all raw energy and boyish charm.

"I escaped the evil sea king!" He turns and blows a raspberry at Feliks, who has made admirably swift progress up the beach given he's bringing three small children with him.

"Rahh! Foiled again!" Feliks roars, then lunges for Ezra, who just about manages to dodge out of the way, but then circles back to join the fun as Feliks grabs the other kids who have attempted to escape while he went for Ezra, and tickles them.

I laugh and stroke my bump as they gang up on Feliks and he pretends to collapse at my feet.

He lies in the soft sand, getting totally covered, and grins as Ezra demands another race. Or monster chase. I admit I'm not clear on what game they're playing, but I don't think they are either. It hardly matters.

I have a family I never expected, but love more than anything. My sisters visit the island too, of course, and it's amazing when we're all together, with all the kids. Feliks is still excellent at putting sunscreen onto smaller creatures than himself—though only I get the full treatment including innuendo—and although it's chaotic it's a lot of fun. But I adore spending time with just the six of us.

Soon to be seven. The baby reminds me with another little kick.

"Daddy! Again, again! I want you to be the Mer-king again!" Kaia says, bouncing with the extraordinary energy of a five-year-old.

"My queen, please, call off your guards, I give in," he begs, eyes full of mirth as he looks at me. Then his gaze dips to my rounded belly and his expression softens to an affectionate smile.

"My king, you just have to say the word," I tease.

"Is the word ice-cream?" he says, and the kids erupt into pleading, questions about what flavours they get for winning, and happy squeals.

Feliks takes all the kids to wash off the sand in the sea, then returns to help me to my feet, running his hands down my sides and over my belly on the pretext of steadying me.

"Can't wait to have you alone," he leans down and whispers in my ear.

I smile up at him, my heart so full of love for this man who has given me everything I wanted and more that I wasn't even aware I needed.

"Ice-cream!" Nova cuts through the romantic moment with a reminder of what I promised.

"Okay!" Feliks laughs as he slings his arm over my shoulders, and we follow the kids into the house to the well-stocked freezer. "Let's see what sweet treats we can all have." Then he whispers into my ear. "And I'll be thinking of the sweetness between your legs that's all *mine*."

EXTENDED EPILOGUE
PAYTON

I'm so sleepy at dinner, I don't even notice Ezra flicking peas at Kaia, and it's Feliks who laughingly leans over and stops Nova from pushing pureed carrot into her ears.

"It's good for your sight, not hearing, rypka, but you have to put into your mouth." He wipes it away, and I'm just about to panic that maybe it's in her ear canal, when Feliks gives me a severe look. "I will deal with it, lisichka."

"I can..." I protest half-heartedly.

His brows lower, and I stop talking.

In truth, I can, but it would be a struggle. We've had an amazing day. I got a solid two hours of kid-free reading time while Feliks played with them, even including the moments when I put my book down because of incoming wet children. But although we have an afternoon siesta when we're here—the heat is too much after lunch—that hasn't prevented me crashing into exhaustion by dinner.

"That's enough, Payton," he growls as I start to get up when everyone's ice-cream bowls are empty and Ezra is asking about being allowed to go and play.

"Daddy!" Kaia says, halfway out of her seat.

He nods understandingly. "You can all play for half an hour, then bathtime."

They all scamper off, except Nova, who raises her arm to be lifted from her high chair. Feliks is there before me, and she toddles towards the sound of laughter from the kids' playroom.

"I'll go and—" I don't even finish my suggestion, because Feliks cuts me off.

"I can see you're tired. You're having a wash and then bed, same as the children." He kneels down beside my chair and reaches possessively for my nape, then slides his hand up and cups my jaw. I relax into it, letting my head flop to the side.

"Sent to bed earlier than the kids," I joke.

He smirks. "They don't have the same demands on them."

"You mean pregnancy?" I rub my hands over my belly. "I love it."

"Mmm. Yes, but I need you, Payton. I'd like it if you were awake, but that's not strictly necessary." His voice is gruff and sends shudders of desire through me. It's a promise and almost a threat.

I adore his touch. I crave it, even now, after so many years together. I love it when he fills me up, makes me feel him inside impossibly deep and leaves me dripping and trembling.

"Go on. Have a shower and go to bed. You can read if you like. Though my baby is doing a good job of wearing you out. But if you do stay up, know that you won't get much sleep once I join you." He leans down and tenderly kisses my forehead. "You could have a bath?"

"I love you," I say impulsively. We tell each other that multiple times a day. I'll never tire of hearing it.

"I love you too," he rumbles. "Now, be a good girl for me and get some rest before your insatiable husband wakes you."

Gratitude swells in my heart. This man. He's a wonderful father and husband. He knows what I need without my asking, be it time to sit and read on the beach, or a command to go to rest, knowing he will do bath and bedtime with the children. He gets away with using the shower in the wet room and spraying each child in turn and the kids think it's so much fun.

He's the perfect balance to me.

"Mummy!" A plaintive cry rises from the playroom.

"Daddy is on his way," Feliks calls and gives me a little push. I hesitate, but he makes an ominous growling noise, and I obey.

In the privacy of Feliks' and my bedroom and en-suite, I undress, and collapse into a bubble bath with my eReader until my eyes are closing.

I hear a cross between a giggle and a screech from the other side of the house, and my inclination to spy on my husband being adorable battles with the fact that our child is weighing me down, and Feliks might frog-march me back to bed, or at least glower at me for not doing as I was told. Besides, when I slip under the sheets, a wave of tiredness takes me, and I fall into the warm, contented darkness.

I awake on my side, moaning, heat behind me. Feliks' hands are on my breasts, cupping and rubbing over my nipples, and his thick, velvet-covered steel cock is pressed between my thighs. He nuzzles my hair.

"Payton." Desire spirals down my spine as he kisses my neck. "I need you."

"Feliks," I whisper, opening my eyes enough to see it's completely dark, then closing them to indulge.

He chuckles as he grasps my upper thigh, pulling me open. "I'm glad you're awake."

The blunt end of his erection presses to the place between my legs where I'm soaked—already? How long has he been doing this?—and nudges meaningfully.

"Mine," he rasps, low, but somehow totally feral. "Take my cock, wife."

There's a stream of words in Russian as he drives into me. There's no hesitation. It's not a question and an answer, it's a claim.

He begins to move inside me immediately, thrusting, his breath harsh as he fucks me. And he continues to speak soft words in his native tongue, as he stretches me out, caressing my breasts until he transfers one hand to my hip to grip me and thrust deeper. Harder.

I once made him tell me what he said when we had sex. It made me blush. Loving words, yes. Over the top statements about how I'm his world, his soul mate, the woman he can't live without.

He's come a long way from that day on the beach when he couldn't say, "I love you."

He can now, but he still says it most fervently when he's buried deep in me.

And he also says depraved, filthy phrases about how he wants to own every part of me. How he wants to cover me with his seed, breed me, fuck my mouth and my cunt, and own every inch of my body.

Crude words. Romantic words. My brain doesn't know the difference. Both make me hot and tingly and wound up.

He pumps into me from behind, adjusting my position on his cock as he likes.

Then his teeth are at my neck, and he bites. Hard enough to hurt, but nowhere near to drawing blood. But it spikes desire in me, a shock that means I'm fully awake now.

I whimper, need making my pussy clench around him.

And like always, I don't have to ask. Feliks just knows.

He shifts one hand to between my legs, slides his fingers through my soaked folds, and strokes in perfect time with the rhythm of his cock.

I'm moaning within seconds.

"Come on my cock, wife," he demands. "I want to feel you, uhhggh…" He trails off as white light explodes from where he's stroking into me and rubbing my clit. He's so solid, and hitting just the right spot, faster as soon as I begin to come, that it's overwhelming.

I feel when he comes, his cock swelling impossibly inside of me and he grunts, shoving himself deeper.

I'm still pulsing when he gathers me even closer to his chest, keeping his cock in me.

"Mine," he breathes.

"Yours." And before long, I'm drifting back into sleep. Happy. Blissed out. Loved.

THANKS

Thank you for reading, I hope you enjoyed it.

Want to read a little more Happily Ever After? Click to get exclusive epilogues and free stories! or head to Evie-RoseAuthor.com

If you have a moment, I'd really appreciate a review wherever you like to talk about books. Reviews, however brief, help readers find stories they'll love.

Love to get the news first? Follow me on your favored social media platform - I love to chat to readers and you get all the latest gossip.

If the newsletter is too much like commitment, I recommend following me on BookBub, where you'll just get new release notifications and deals.

- amazon.com/author/evierose
- bookbub.com/authors/evie-rose
- instagram.com/evieroseauthor
- tiktok.com/@EvieRoseAuthor

I THINK YOU'LL LOVE TO READ THIS NEXT...

Same vibes of instalove, he falls first and knows it, chase, and a wedding.

Seized by the Mafia King

"I'll be taking this."

At the altar, I silently plead for someone to save me from a marriage I don't want.

Then, when the priest asks if anyone objects to this marriage, the church doors are thrown open, a tall, older man with ice-blue eyes and air of casual wealth and power, stalks in, and says, "I'll be taking this."

He carries me out of the church over his shoulder.

Kingpin Zane Bethnal might have saved me, but it turns out, I'm in his debt.

I have no money to pay.

The only thing I can offer him is myself...

A sweet and spicy age gap instalove romance novella, with a jealous and possessive billionaire mafia boss and his untouched bride...

MORE SPICY READS BY EVIE ROSE

Grumpy Bosses

Older Hotter Grumpier

My billionaire boss catches me reading when I should be working. And the punishment...?

Tall, Dark, and Grumpy

When my boss comes to fetch me from a bar, I'm expecting him to go nuts that I'm drunk and described my fake boyfriend just like him. But he demands marriage.

Silver Fox Grump

When your dad's best friend is teaching you to kiss, and says, "I can't breathe without you."

Obsessed Bratva Bosses

Bratva's Secret Girl

She's my secret obsession. Then they find her.

Bratva's Stolen Bride

My boyfriend's dad kidnapped me, and forced me to marry him.

Bratva's Forbidden Love

One night with a mafia boss.

Stalker Kingpins

Spoiled by my Stalker

From the moment we lock eyes, I'm his lucky girl... But there's a price to pay

Kingpin's Baby

I beg the Kingpin for help... And he offers marriage.

Owned by her Enemy

I didn't expect the ruthless new kingpin—an older man, gorgeous and hard—to extract such a price for a ceasefire: an arranged marriage.

His Public Claim

My first time is sold to my brother's best friend

Accidentally Kidnapping the Mafia Boss

I might have kidnapped him, but the mafia boss isn't going to let me go.

Marrying the Boss

Baby Proposal

My boss walked in on me buying "magic juice" online... And now he's demanding to be my baby's daddy!

Groom Gamble

I wanted a baby, but I never dreamed my grumpy boss would be the daddy!

London Mafia Bosses

Captured by the Mafia Boss

I might be an innocent runaway, but I'm at my friend's funeral to avenge her murder by the mafia boss: King.

Taken by the Kingpin

Tall, dark, older and dangerous, I shouldn't want him.

Stolen by the Mafia King

I had a plan to escape. Everything is going perfectly at my wedding rehearsal dinner until *he* turns up.

Caught by the Kingpin

The kingpin growls a warning that I shouldn't try his patience by attempting to escape.

Claimed by the Mobster

I'm in love with my ex-boyfriend's dad: a dangerous and powerful mafia boss twice my age.

Snatched by the Bratva

I have an excruciating crush on this man who comes into the coffee shop. Every day. He's older, gorgeous, perfectly dressed. He has a Russian accent and silver eyes.

Kidnapped by the Mafia Boss

A tall dark rescuer crashed through the door… and kidnapped me.

Held by the Bratva

"Who hurt you?"

Seized by the Mafia King

I'm kidnapped from my wedding

Abducted by the Mafia Don

"Touch her and die."

Nabbed by the Bratva

"If I catch you, I keep you. Now run."

Filthy Scottish Kingpins

Forbidden Appeal

He's older and rich, and my teenage crush re-surfaces as I beg the former kingpin to help me escape a mafia arranged marriage. He stares at me like I'm a temptress he wants to banish, but we're snowed in at his Scottish castle.

Captive Desires

I was sent to kill him, but he's captured me, and I'm at his mercy. He says he'll let me go if I beg him to take his…

Eager Housewife

Her best friend's dad is advertising for a free use convenient housewife, and she's the perfect applicant.

Protective Kingpins

Kingpin's Nanny

My grumpy boss bought my whole evening as a camgirl!

Printed in Dunstable, United Kingdom